CRIME SYNDICATE MAGAZINE

ISSUE THREE, OCTBOER 2017
A MAGAZINE OF CRIME FICTION

Edited by
Eryk Pruitt with Michael Pool

WWW.CRIMESYNDICATEMAGAZINE.COM

Crime Syndicate Magazine
ISSUE THREE, OCTOBER 2017

Cover photo by Stephanie Pool
Cover design by Michael Pool
Formatting by Rik – Wild Seas Formatting
(http://www.WildSeasFormatting.com)

eBook ISBN: 978-0-9968552-9-7
Print ISBN: 978-0-9968552-8-0

WWW.CRIMESYNDICATEMAGAZINE.COM

WHAT WE RECKON

International Book Tour

OCT 7	NOIR AT THE BAR	WONDERLAND BALLROOM	WASHINGTON, DC
OCT 9	BOOK LAUNCH	REGULATOR BOOKSHOP	DURHAM, NC
OCT 12-16	BOUCHERCON	MARRIOTT HOTEL	TORONTO, CANADA
NOV 3	BOOK SIGNING	INTERABANG BOOKS	DALLAS, TX
NOV 4	NOIR AT THE BAR	TBA	AUSTIN, TX
NOV 6	BOOK SIGNING	BOOKPEOPLE	AUSTIN, TX
NOV 7	BOOK SIGNING	MURDER BY THE BOOK	HOUSTON, TX
NOV 9	NOIR AT THE BAR	WILD DETECTIVES	DALLAS, TX
NOV 17	NOIR AT THE BAR	ROGUE TAVERN	BIRMINGHAM, AL
DEC 7	NOIR AT THE BAR	106 MAIN	DURHAM, NC

ERYK PRUITT

www.erykpruitt.com

i

A note from the Editor's Desk:

Well hello there, friends and partners in crime. Been a while. It's my fault. Life got crazy, or hectic, or terrifying, whatever terminology you prefer. The magazine was forced to suffer my personal transition in silence, which was not my preference, but was necessary regardless.

It's been two states, sixteen months, and more booze, coffee, and confusion than I would have thought possible since the last installment of Crime Syndicate Magazine hit shelves. Casting myself as ecstatic being back to publishing bad-ass crime fiction short stories is miles shy of how I feel right now.

The good news is, Crime Syndicate is back ... in black, you might say. And we've brought friends for the storytelling fun. Chief among those friends is our Guest Editor, Eryk Pruitt, one of the very best southern noir authors writing today, and just one hell of a guy in general.

We've also got stories from nine other crime writers who are so ferocious, so atrocious, and so straight-up talented we don't deserve them in our pages.

So, without wasting another moment dwelling on the past, let's just dive right into what is sure to be the future of crime fiction. And what a future it is, every bit as bright as it will be dark. Cheers, until next time. God willing that time will come sooner than later, but no guarantees.

--Michael Pool, Editor and Founder, Crime Syndicate Magazine

Contents

The Deplorables

Eryk Pruitt

YOU'RE TIRED.

Beat and tired and ready for that no-count husband of yours to get off the toilet so you can use it. Or for that kid of yours to wake and dress himself for school and do it quick, because if he misses the bus and you got to drive him, there'll be hell to pay. Hell to pay for him and for you, if you're late to work again.

You didn't get to bed until damn near three-thirty last night because your husband Trigger was in another of his moods. The kind he gets from time to time and the only light at the end of that tunnel is a bottle of corn liquor and, before it will knock him cold to the floor, you have to put up with two hours of his hooting and hollering, but it sure beats the alternative.

So you finish your cigarette and stub it to the ashtray, slather butter on a couple of stale biscuits and scrape the last of the scrambled eggs to the plate, then call upstairs again for the boy. Warn him he's got five minutes or you're coming up after him. You'd fix yourself another cup of coffee, but Trigger drained the last of it before stepping upstairs to monopolize the shitter. Instead, you fall into a chair at the kitchen table and spend the next four-and-a-half minutes staring at your own toes.

Then down the stairs comes Trigger, still wearing what he had on last night, right down to the mirrored sunglasses and cowboy shirt. He drops into a chair and eyeballs the plate you've set aside for your son. You scoot it a couple inches further from him.

"You'd steal food from a boy with Asperger's?"

"For the last time, he ain't got Asperger's." He reaches across the table with his fork and spears a chunk of yellowed egg. "That's some shit you say when you get sad. Back in my day, they called it being an asshole, not Asperger's."

You say: "I swear, Trigger Raywood, if you say that shit one more time, I'm liable to take that fork from you and poke out both your eyeballs." You mean it, too. There is a short list of things your husband can do to get you riled and he knows each and every one of them. "You and me read the same articles on the internet. You know good and well what kind of breaks they get in school when it's time to apply for colleges, don't you?"

"What's got you all worked up?" he asks.

"The fact that you don't know speaks volumes, Trigger."

You leave him to work it out for himself while you call up for the boy one last time. Behind you: the scraping of a fork against plate. This weight sinking your shoulders feels like a load of hot, wet towels. You turn to give him the business, but nearly trip over a cleat in the middle of the floor and you stop, wondering for the life of you to whom it belongs.

"Trigger," you say, with a calmness that surprises even you, "I need you to do me a favor today."

"Not today," he says, mouth full of toast. "I got to run out to Diboll and pick up that solvent I was telling you about."

"What solvent?"

His voice raises an exasperated octave. "The one I was telling you about. Didn't you hear a word I was saying last night?"

You honestly can't remember a thing y'all talked about last night. He'd come home rubbing his nose this way and that, swearing he ain't touched any blow, but you know better. You know better by the way he's sniffing and chewing his lower lip. By how he's sucked air through his nose and it rattles all the way back to the bottom of his throat like a mud flap. He don't talk that fast when he ain't doing blow. You get revenge by sneaking off to the bathroom and touching a little of your own. Lie right back to him.

But the joke is on you this morning.

"What on earth are you talking about, Trigger?"

"For the carpet cleaner," he says. "Floor mats. The stuff that goes in the XB-100." The question mark on your face must have spoken volumes because he throws up his hands again and says, "The carpet cleaner Raymond said he'd lend me."

"For floor mats?"

"Jesus Christ, Becca." He drops his fork to the table, where it clatters off the side and hits the floor. He doesn't move to pick it up. "What's the point of staying up all night to tell you my hopes and dreams if you ain't going to remember none of it the next morning?"

"If your dreaming didn't come with a halfgallon of brown liquor and god knows what all else …"

But you don't get to finish because in comes the boy. He's still half asleep, but dressed and ready. He shuffles to the fridge to take a look inside, but you have no idea why because it's got just as much or as little shit as it did the night before, when last he looked. He shuts the door, then shuffles to the sink to fish out a glass clean enough to drink from.

"You better not miss your bus," you tell him. You tell him again, because he doesn't seem to hear you the first time. Then, because he's got difficulties, you tell him once more.

"I know," grunts the boy, before stomping out of the kitchen to gather his things and wait by the door. You wish you were still in bed. Covers over your head. You wish for once Trigger would fuss with the boy in the mornings because, if you could do it all over again, you'd insist he wear a rubber.

No. Don't say that. You don't mean it.

"Trigger … Without raising your voice … Could you please tell me what this TB-600 whatever is used for? Why you got to go all the way to Diboll this afternoon of all afternoons?"

Trigger uses the butter knife to free mud from the tread of his work boots. It drops to the floor and explodes into tiny clodlets of dirt, each one fine and dandy to stay there until kingdom come. He doesn't bother to look up as he speaks.

"You got to ask yourself one question, Becca," he says. "Do you want to live like this the rest of your life, or do you want things to get better?"

You don't dare open your mouth for fear of the fury that may spring forth. In fact, you burrow deep those upper teeth of yours into your lower lip until you find something new to get your goat. Down the street, you hear the telltale whistle of the brakes on the school bus and you see the boy has yet to move from the doorway. You shout at him louder than necessary and ask him why in the hell he ain't run down to the bus stop yet.

"I hate you!" he screams. "I hate both of you and one day I'm going to make you both sorry you were such assholes!"

You don't know what you'd do if you caught him. He's too fast and you're too tired and there's too much clutter. He's out the door and down the sidewalk. You stare after him from the doorway, happy for now that he's boarded the bus and on the way to school where he can do no harm.

"Like you said," says Trigger. "Asperger's."

You sigh. You turn to face your husband and you want to scream, scream loud and long with every inclination to shatter all the windows in the house, but then where would you be? You have no idea when this happened. It could have been yesterday, if it hadn't felt like forever. But it wasn't forever, because you can remember it. You can almost taste it. Trips to the beach. Sitting at the Whataburger with the girls. Hoping Trigger would come around because tonight might be the night you let him …

You find your hand inside the whatnot drawer. What in the hell are you fishing out of there? A screwdriver? What would you do with that? You hate the way coke does your head the morning after. You don't think clear. Not like the level-headed member of the family is supposed to think. If it weren't for the coke, you're certain you wouldn't have your hand in the whatnot drawer, holding tight to a screwdriver and …

Then you see it, that fucking pen.

How you haven't wanted to be reminded of that pen or what you did to get it, so you tucked it away in the whatnot drawer with the screwdriver and used dishrags and little packets of soy sauce from the chink joint up the road. You stare at it longer than necessary and become acutely aware of how fast or slow your reaction time really is.

"Trigger," you say, picking up the pen, "you ain't going to Diboll today. You're going to come with me on an errand and you ain't giving me no sass either."

***

Folks around these parts have known for years that when it comes to getting something, you need go no further than that dude named Kind. They got stores up and down the highways stretching from Longview to Houston, but there's plenty things can't be found in stores. Plenty things folks want and maybe even need, but won't be nowhere near any shelves or found on sale. No, that's where a dude named Kind factors into everyday life.

But even Kind has to get his shit from somewhere and there weren't no telling what folks might come offering or even what folks might reckon he'll need. Usually, it's drugs. As far as the dude named Kind knows, marijuana grows on trees. Coke, too. Every couple of years or so, heroin will come around again, but mostly these days, it's legal drugs. Legal if you have a prescription, at least. And with all the colleges in the area, he runs a pretty decent trade in things requiring a prescription.

You don't like the look on his face when he opens the door. His eyes go to yours, then head elsewhere. Eventually, they make their way over to your husband, but then go right back to where they'd been stationed previous.

"Kind," you say. "How are you doing?"

"Better now," he says. He opens the door wider. "Y'all come on in."

You do, Trigger close behind. Kind's apartment is in much better shape than your own place and right away you want to give Trigger a piece of your mind. Sure, Kind is half full of stepped-on East Texas crystal, but often times so is Trigger, so why can't he clean the place up? Pick up his socks at least? You come on inside and stand near the couch, wait to be told to sit.

You notice Kind has yet to take his eyes rimmed-red off the hem of your shorts. The ones cut to right about the middle of a thigh that bulges more than it used to. Kind's gotten lost in it and his mouth hangs a touch slack.

"Kind?"

"I sure would like to bite that," says Kind.

Against your better judgement, you ask, "You sure would like to bite what?"

"That." He points to your thigh, swelling just beneath your shorts.

"Why on earth would you want to bite it?"

He smiles. "Because it looks delicious."

Finally, up steps Trigger. He raises his hand like maybe he'll hail a cab.

"Dude," he says, "that's my wife."

"Then you know what I'm talking about," says Kind. He considers the matter settled. He unpauses the video game on the giant flat screen against the wall and resumes playing. Over his shoulder, he says, "You want to spit it out, or would you rather I dive in after it?"

You waste no time. You reach into your pocket and fish out a handkerchief. You hold it high.

"What we got is this here pen," you say. To confirm that Kind's hearing had, in fact, not gone shitty, you carefully unwrap the handkerchief — gingerly, so as not to smudge or break it — and unfurl a gilded click pen, about as thick as two of your fingers. You turn it around and around in your hand. "Do you want to hold it?"

"What the fuck does it matter if I want to hold it?" asks Kind. "I don't care anything about no pen."

"This ain't just any pen," you say. "Me and Trigger stole this pen out of William Faulkner's house. You know who William Faulkner is, don't you?"

Kind looks at you both rather suspiciously. "How the hell did you get into William Faulkner's house?"

"It's a museum," Trigger says. "Anybody can get into it."

"We took one of those tours and when weren't anybody looking, we stole the pen." You can't force the smile from your face as Kind pauses the video game again and drops the controller to his feet. He turns to face you both. "And now we brought it to you."

"I ain't got no use for a pen," he says. He turns back to the flat screen, but doesn't pick up the controller.

"But it's the pen William Faulkner used when he wrote his greatest classics," you say. "Trigger, tell Kind some of the books he wrote with this pen."

"*Of Mice and Men* and *The Sun Also Rises*," Trigger says.

"I'm pretty sure he used a typewriter," says Kind. "And besides, what the hell would I do with a pen used by some writer? It probably doesn't even work anymore."

"Oh, it works," says Trigger. "It works real good. Trust me, I used it."

Kind eyeballs the pen. "What did you do with it?"

"I wrote a story," says Trigger. "At least, I wrote the beginning of one. Hell, I wrote the beginning of seven of them."

"But you didn't finish none of them?"

Quick as the lash, you say, "He may not have finished one, but he sure as fire started them and, let me tell you, when they finally do get finished … Boy howdy."

Trigger takes a seat on the couch, though didn't nobody ask him to. You stay right where you are. That look in Kind's eye says he ain't decided yet if he's going for it. A good piece of you wishes Trigger would shut the hell up. A good piece of you reckons if you hadn't brought him along, you'd have already sold the damn pen by now.

To confirm your suspicions, Trigger says, "No, I didn't finish them, but it don't matter because I ain't never started seven stories before I got this here pen. That's how I know it works."

"So what do you say?" you ask. "Two hundred bucks?"

"Two hundred bucks for a pen?" Kind kicks the video game controller across the floor and narrows the distance between you and he. You get every notion he probably would have slapped some sense into you and came about a hair short of doing so. But he seems to gather his wits about him. He looks you up and down, and this time you're fine with it because it appears to calm him some and you really want him calmed.

Kind says: "You know, I entertained you this far because you and me got history, Becca, but I have to say Al McGuire warned me about getting mixed up with this one here."

Trigger looks like he might go buckwild at the mere mention of Al McGuire. If there's one thing he's still touchy about, it's that mess with Al McGuire and six feet of dirt on top of that bastard won't cool him none over it. So Trigger's up and shouting and this gets Kind all indignant because he won't be talked to like that in his own house and he starts spouting this and that, and you have no doubt in a contest over who can make who angrier, Kind is liable to say some things you'd rather Trigger not know about. And you know for a fact that Kind has a forty-four tucked somewhere in his bedroom along with god-knows-what-all else.

"Maybe a long time ago, I would have paid a girl like you two hundred bucks for a pen," says Kind, "but them days are long past and I blame this bastard right here." He points a crooked finger toward Trigger. "He done ruined what fruit once tasted sweet and good and for what? Tell me that, Becca. For what?"

And you sigh.

You sigh because you don't know if he's right or wrong. You sigh because you've had it up to here with all of them. You sigh because every which way you look, whether you take the high road or the low one, either way your clothes end up just as sullied, so you pick up that big, overflowing crystal ashtray and brain the fucker, which drops him straight to the floor.

Kind, that is.

Trigger, on the other hand, ain't quite clear what to say. Both of you look down at the floor and see Kind. He ain't moving. He ain't moving an inch other than the steady stream of purple blood running out the back of his head and a phantom twitch at that bony, grey finger of his, still pointing at your husband.

"What the hell, honey?"

"Oh sure," you say. "Go ahead and put this one on me, will you."

Trigger scratches fast at his head. He opens and closes his mouth. He does this a good while until finally he spits it out.

"Babe," he says, "how's he supposed to fetch us the money for the pen if you done hauled off and killed him?"

Bless his heart, that husband of yours. It ain't his fault, entirely. You blame his parents. His upbringing. They went without for so long, they wouldn't and couldn't know a way out if it looked them dead in the eye.

You? You're different.

And your children will be different.

You'll make sure of it because, as you look around Kind's apartment at the cash, the weed, the coke, the pills — hell, the two M-16s on yonder kitchen table — you and yours may never again know want, if you play it proper. With money like that, you could set yourself up nice and solid.

With money like that, you think, as you drum your fingers across your pregnant belly, you just might not have a single reason to get rid of it after all.

Good Cop Bad Cop

Kevin Z. Garvey

"AM I BEING DETAINED?" said the driver of the late model BMW. "Am I free to go?"

I smiled. Here we go again, I thought. Another YouTube constitutionalist, thinking he knew his rights.

"License and registration, please," I said, nice and polite. I always start off polite. The good cop.

"I asked if I was being *detained*," the driver said. "I know my rights." He gestured toward the cell phone in a stand mounted to his dashboard, pointed at me. "I'm recording this interaction, by the way. Which is also within my rights."

I just stared at the guy. What a weasel. His ride cost more than my annual salary. The smirk on his face begged to be wiped off. Patience, I told myself. Patience.

"You were doing thirty in a twenty-five

zone," I said.

"You pulled me over for that? Are you kidding me?"

"License and registration," I said again. No please this time. Still in good cop mode, but feeling the first tingles of the bad cop rising in me.

We eyeballed each other for a few seconds before he took out his wallet and produced his license. I took it from him and waited for the registration. Kept my eyes on him as he reached into the glove box, my hand poised on my service weapon, because sometimes they come out with something other than the reggie. But not this time. He handed me the papers. I looked them over. His name was Alex Austin.

"Be right back," I said, intending to take the documents to my prowler and look him up.

As I turned to walk away, he said, "Hey."

I turned back. "Yeah?"

"You know, when I was a kid, around ten years old, I wanted to be a cop."

I shrugged.

"But then I turned eleven."

I stood there, looking at him. "You done?"

"I guess some kids never grow up," he said. "That's gotta suck."

"It's a living," I said.

"Nah," Austin said. "More to it than that. You never grew up, that's the real reason. You're still a kid. A pretty big one, though. What are you, six-four, five? But inside you still feel small, huh?

Tiny. Like a little kid, bent over your daddy's knee. Did your old man bully you as a child? Is that why you're a cop?"

I don't know why, but this guy was really getting under my skin. I could feel my face getting hot, was glad the red lights from my flashers were on to cover up the color that had to be rising in my cheeks.

"Go on now, Mr. Big Man with the little dick," Austin went on, oblivious to the danger he was in. "Run back to your crappy little squad car and write me up. Gotta meet your quota, right? Maybe your captain will give you a gold star right before he fucks you in the ass, like your daddy used to do."

It was then that something snapped in my head. A wave of calm poured over me, like warm water. I stood there, staring into his eyes. At peace.

"What are you waiting for?" he said. "Hurry up, asshole. You're on my dime. My taxes pay your salary."

"Okay," I said, my voice pleasant, without a trace of heat. "Let me run your plates. If they come up clean, I'll let you off with a warning."

Austin looked at me like I had two heads. "Seriously?"

"Seriously. Not all cops are assholes."

He didn't know what to say.

"But first," I said, pointing to a spot in the road ahead of him, "I need you to pull your car up a few feet and park it a little better, okay? The nose is kind of out in the street. You don't want someone coming along and denting your ride."

Austin's demeanor began to change. It was like he couldn't really believe what he was hearing. I could tell he was happy about not getting a ticket. He probably had a lot of points on his license as it was.

"About ten, twenty feet is good," I said. "I'll be right back."

I went back to my prowler. As I climbed in, the BMW's engine started. My dashboard camera was recording. I tugged on the audio cable, unplugging it but leaving the video on.

He started to move. I smiled as I flicked on my siren and mashed the pedal. Bolting out in front of his car, I made a sharp right in front of him, blocking him in.

Now my camera was in front of his car, recording nothing but empty road. And the audio was dead. I was invisible.

I killed the siren, hopped out of the prowler, and walked back to Austin. He was sitting in his car, staring at me, a look of concern on his face. I ripped open the door, grabbed him by his collar and yanked him from the car, sending him sprawling on his ass in the road.

"Yes, you *are* being detained, you rat motherfucker," I said, bad cop in full effect. "You are *not* free to go."

"I'll have your badge!" he roared.

I pulled my weapon and pointed it at him. "The only thing you're having is a funeral, shithead."

I squeezed off three shots, right into his chest. Bam! Bam! Bam! A nice tight grouping. He wheezed, then went silent. I'd purposely avoided shooting him in the face because I wanted to see if the smirk would follow him into the afterlife. It didn't. He died with his mouth open, like the bitch he was.

I stared at him for a few seconds, enjoying the sense of release I felt, like the afterglow of a busted nut. Then I holstered my weapon and got busy. Reaching down, I unsnapped my ankle holster and took out my drop gun. I always carried one with me for situations like this, though I'd never had to use it before. My other shootings had all been legit.

I kneeled down and pressed Austin's fingertips onto the gun, leaving his prints all over it. Then I wrapped his forefinger around the trigger, aimed high and fired, twice. The bullets sailed into the night. After that I picked up the piece and threw it, to justify my own fingerprints being on it.

There. I'd covered my ass. Now it was time to call in the cavalry. I hit the talk button on my shoulder radio. "Shots fired!" I shouted. "Shots fired!"

As I waited for reinforcements to arrive, I went back to the BMW and used a tissue to pluck

Austin's cell phone from its stand. I carried it back to where he was sprawled on his back, deader than shit. I placed the phone on his chest, over his shirt pocket. Then I stood over him and gave the camera a middle-finger salute.

"No more YouTube for you, douchebag," I said as I aimed my service weapon. I fired a shot at the phone and hit it. Bull's-eye. The round went right through, into the dead man's chest. So much for recording his interactions with the police. Using the tissue, I picked up the demolished phone and tucked it into Austin's pocket.

By now I could hear sirens in the distance. I radioed in again, trying to sound panicked, telling the dispatcher to send an ambulance. Then I went back to the prowler, sat in the driver's seat and practiced acting shook up.

***

As is customary with police shootings, I got a paid vacation out of it. The investigation always takes time, and eventually you either get cleared or charged. The union kept me abreast of things, and for the first week or so everything seemed to be going my way. That's why, when Captain Reynolds called and asked me to come down to the station, I didn't think twice about it. In fact, I thought I was being cleared and that they were going to give me back my gun.

"Hey, Cap," I said, when I got there.

He was sitting behind his desk. There were a

couple of guys in civilian clothes in the office with him. I didn't recognize either one of them. They looked like detectives, but I didn't know for sure. One of them was sitting in a chair in front of the captain's desk, the other on the couch along the wall. I didn't like the way they were eyeballing me.

"Big Jake," Reynolds said. "Thanks for coming down." He gestured at the empty seat in front of his desk.

I sat down, and the guy next to me stood up and moved towards the door. I watched as he took up a position in the doorway, like he was blocking it. I knew right then I was fucked.

I turned back to Reynolds. "What's going on, Cap? Who are these guys?"

"Jake, listen. I've got bad news." He picked up a remote and pointed with it at the mounted TV in his office. "Watch."

He hit a button on the remote and video began to roll.

I saw my own face, with a crazed expression on it.

I watched myself flip the bird.

"No more YouTube for you, douchebag," I heard myself say.

There was a flash. The screen went black.

I sat there, stunned, wondering how in the hell they'd salvaged that video from the phone.

"That was just the ending," Reynolds said. "Would you like to see it from the beginning?"

I shook my head, still too shocked to speak.

"Alex Austin had his phone streaming video," Reynolds said. "His computer at home saved a copy. One of his family members found it."

The guy on the couch stood up. "Internal Affairs," he said. "You're under arrest."

So they were dicks, after all. Here to take me to jail.

Captain Reynolds said, "You're not armed, are you, Jake?"

I made a face. "If I was, I'd already have wasted these two pricks."

"Take it easy, Jake," Reynolds told me. "Don't make things worse."

I stood up, feeling panic in my gut. I thought about bolting. About running right over the guy in the doorway. But I knew it was no use. I was fucked. There was no escape. I put my hands behind my head and laced my fingers.

"Do what you gotta do," I said.

***

My bail hearing was a circus. A snippet of the video had been leaked to the press, enough to cause a minor sensation. The courtroom was packed. My mother was there, too, and it pained me to see the devastated look on her face. The judge denied bail. No surprise there. The case against me was too strong. Overwhelming. You didn't have to be a law scholar to know I was looking at the death penalty. The judge set a date for the arraignment, one week hence.

They took me to a cell in protective custody. I was alone, isolated from the other prisoners. If you've never experienced that kind of solitude, in a tiny, oppressive cell with no links to the outside world, there's no way to understand it. It's pathological boredom. Torture.

I tried to sleep some of the tedium away, but no luck. When you're desperate to sleep, that's when you can't. Reading helped a little, but not much, because every time I looked up from the page I'd see my filthy cell and come crashing back to reality. I spent a lot of time kicking myself in the ass for allowing Alex Austin to get the better of me. I replayed the events of that fateful night over and over in my head, thinking about all the opportunities I had to walk away. But there was just something about the guy. I didn't want to walk away. I wanted to kill that cocksucker, and I had. And I'd enjoyed it.

Still, I wished I could have found it within myself not to lose my cool during my encounter with him. For my mother's sake. At the bail hearing she'd been distraught. I felt terrible for her, having to see her only child in jail, accused of murder, with overwhelming evidence to back up the charge. It made me wonder how many years I'd taken off her life.

On a positive family note, my father was long dead. I was glad that he wasn't around to see me in that courtroom. Because now I wouldn't have to see him gloat. Years ago, when I told him I'd taken the test to become a cop, he laughed and said there was no way I'd pass. But I did pass, and entered the academy. Then he predicted I'd wash out in the first week. Wrong again, pops. I graduated.

Finally, he assured me that I'd never make it through probation. And once again he was dead wrong, though he never knew it, having kicked the bucket three months before my probie period ended. For a time I felt cheated about that, resentful that I couldn't rub his nose in it. But now I was grateful that he was gone.

Thinking of my father made me wonder how things might have turned out between me and my own son, if I'd had one. But in my situation, I was glad I didn't have kids. It would have sucked for them to know that their dad was facing the needle. I didn't have a wife either, or a girlfriend for that matter, so no one came to visit me except for my slimy lawyer, Jerry Binder, Esq.

"You're in serious trouble," Binder told me. "That video is very incriminating."

"Gee, ya think," I said. "Is there any way you can get me off?"

He shook his head. "No."

"Then what am I paying you for?"

"You're not paying me. I was appointed by the court. But even the most expensive lawyer in the world wouldn't be able to beat this charge.

The best we can do is try and save your life."

There it was. The harsh reality. "How?"

"By copping a plea. The victim's family has seen the video. They don't want it released. They're embarrassed at the way the victim spoke to you. I believe they'd be fine with dropping the capital charge in exchange for not having a trial. A guilty plea would put you in prison for life without the possibility of parole, but you'd keep your life."

Even though I somehow knew that this would be how things ended up, I still couldn't grasp what I was hearing. I sat there, stunned.

"A trial would be very high profile," Binder said. "And your chances of winning virtually nil."

He was right, of course. Considering how much of a clown show the bail hearing had been, I couldn't even imagine the three-ring circus a trial would bring. Even worse, every day in court I would have to sit there, watching my mother wither away.

"Looks like I've got no choice," I said.

"Afraid not."

I shrugged. "Fuck it, then. Plead."

***

A month later I was on a bus heading for my new home, the state penitentiary, where I'd live out my years until the day I died. None of the other prisoners on the bus seemed to recognize me, which was a relief. As a so-called dirty cop in the joint, the last thing you want is for that fact to be known by the cons. It would guarantee a shank with your name on it.

During orientation they gave me a choice: protective custody or general population. I chose gen pop. Not because I'm a people person. I'm not. But I'd already experienced a month of protective custody. I couldn't imagine doing that for decades. I'd rather take the death penalty. Or a shiv in the back.

I acclimated quickly. You have no choice. Not if you want to survive. No one seemed to recognize my name or my face. All they knew was that I was some big surly guy in for murder, and so I was pretty much left alone. I wasn't sure how long that would last, but I hoped for the best.

By chance I had my cell to myself for the first three days of my incarceration. The guy I was supposed to share it with hung himself the night before I arrived. Lucky me. It was stressful waiting for a new cellmate. I had no idea who I would be bunking with, and wasn't looking forward to finding out. The worrying kept me up at night. I wondered if I'd ever get a good night's sleep in this place.

On the evening of day four, he arrived. I had to smile when they brought him in, because he looked a little like Alex Austin, minus the smirk. He was small and skinny, and way out of his element. I felt relieved that he wasn't some hulking bruiser with a chip on his shoulder — like me.

The guy was nervous as shit. He didn't look at me at all for the first hour, which pissed me off.

"You're gonna have to look at me eventually," I said.

His mousey eyes darted around, landed on mine for a split second and then darted away again.

"I'm Jake," I said.

"Ben," he said meekly.

"What are you in for, Benny?"

His voice was a whisper. "I killed … I killed my wife."

I laughed. I don't know why. Just the way he said it.

"Well, good for you," I said.

At that moment it occurred to me that, all things considered, I was pretty lucky. This guy was going to be a decent cellmate. I decided to have some fun.

Using my best good cop voice, I said, "Listen, Benny, since we're gonna be cellies for a long time, a lot of years, we may as well get used to it. I mean, we're living together, right? That makes us family."

He nodded and seemed to be calming down a little. He even maintained eye contact for longer than a split second.

"So we're cool?" I said.

He nodded again. "Yeah."

"Family?"

He looked at me and even managed a smile. "Sure," he said. "Family, yeah."

"Great," I said. "And now, since we're a family, we have a decision to make. We have to decide which one of us is the mommy and which one is the daddy. I'll let you choose."

Benny was still looking at me, but the smile was gone. He looked confused. "What?"

"Our family," I said. "You. The mommy or the daddy?"

He shook his head, like he didn't want to answer. But that wasn't an option.

"Benny, listen to me," I said, my voice changing, no longer the good cop. "You have to choose. I'm not gonna ask you again. Do you want to be the mommy or do you want to be the daddy?"

Benny spread his hands in a gesture of helplessness and squeaked out his answer. "The daddy, I guess?"

"You got it, daddy," I said, smiling. Then, in my most authoritative bad cop voice, I added, "Now get down on your fucking knees, crawl over here, and suck mommy's dick."

In all honesty, I expected him to laugh. It was a joke. An old joke. I don't know how in the world he'd never heard it before. But the look on his face was priceless.

He stared at me for a minute, his bottom lip quivering, like he was about to cry. Then, as if in slow motion, he dropped to his knees. I couldn't believe what I was seeing. As he began to crawl to me I realized that prison life, like everything else, is what you make of it.

He was about two feet away when I decided to let him off the hook. By kicking him in the face. It was a good shot. Sent a tooth flying.

"Not tonight," I said. "Mommy's got a headache."

I don't think he heard me. He seemed to be knocked out. But he recovered pretty quick. Moaning, he pawed at his busted mouth.

I stepped over him to get to my bunk. "Goodnight, daddy," I said as I climbed into bed. Pulling up the covers, I put my head down on the pillow and closed my eyes.

And then, for the first time in what seemed like forever, I slept like a baby.

Below The Angels

Max Booth III

1.

THE CLERK BEHIND THE COUNTER had his hands raised and kept begging not to be killed, saying that he was too young to die, saying he had a family who loved him and a girl he couldn't leave. He was just beginning life, he said—there was no way he could die right now.

All Tommy could say in response was *shut up, shut the fuck up.*

Nikki was pregnant. If Tommy didn't keep reminding himself of that, he'd lose focus and everything would come collapsing down upon him. The gun trembled in his hand and he was afraid he would accidentally pull the trigger.

He was doing this for Nikki. Nikki and the baby they had made together. He couldn't forget about the baby. He couldn't take care of a baby without a job, and no job wanted to hire him, so that didn't leave many options.

He slapped the barrel of the gun against the clerk's face and gasped as blood erupted from the poor guy's nose. The gun was heavy and powerful. He had to be careful or he might end up killing the guy.

The clerk held his face and cried. Tommy waved the gun in front of him and screamed, "OPEN THE FUCKING SAFE AND PUT THE MONEY IN THE BAG OR I SWEAR TO FUCKING GOD, I'LL BLOW YOUR FUCKING BRAINS OUT!"

The clerk scrambled to the floor, hands shaking as he fumbled with the safe underneath the register. As Tommy waited, the front entrance of the drugstore opened and a man in a police uniform strolled inside, whistling without a care in the world.

The cop froze when he saw Tommy standing there pointing a gun at the clerk behind the counter. He stood staring at Tommy, and Tommy stood staring at the cop. Tommy's heart pounded so fast and hard he thought it would crack his sternum open.

"Shit," Tommy said.

The cop reached for his gun and said, "Put that weapon down immediately and …"

Tommy shot him.

Once, right in the gut.

The cop stayed in place for a moment, then

looked down at his bleeding stomach. He looked back at Tommy, shocked. Tommy wondered why the cop had to come into the drugstore right then. Maybe for something to drink, maybe for baby aspirin for his child.

Tommy found himself thinking about children a lot lately.

He pulled the trigger again and this time he missed. The glass door behind the cop exploded and an alarm erupted. He steadied himself and tried again. A new bullet turned the cop's neck into a gory mess and he finally fell down.

"Shit," Tommy said. "Shit, shit, shit."

He jumped over the counter and pushed the traumatized clerk out of the way, shoveling the money into the bag himself. As he turned to leave, he looked back down at the clerk.

"I don't want to kill you," he told him.

"Then … then don't. Please."

"Well, I sure as hell can't leave you here."

"Why not?"

"Too many loose ends," Tommy said. "That's how they catch you."

"Please," the clerk sobbed. "It wasn't supposed to happen like this."

Tommy knelt down and pressed the gun against the clerk's head. He squeezed the trigger. Wet brain matter splattered against his pants.

"Shit," he said again. He fled the drugstore.

Outside, he dove into his Bronco and twisted the key in the ignition. The engine turned over, caught, then sputtered and died. When he tried turning the key again, it didn't even give a courtesy cough.

"Fuck, not now," Tommy screamed, punching the steering wheel. Starting his shitty car was always a gamble. He sat a moment trying to calm his heartbeat, then attempted the engine again. Still nothing.

He heard sirens in the distance. He pounded the steering wheel some more, then got out and ran back into the store. He dug the keys out of the cop's pocket and ran for the squad car parked at the store's entrance. It started with no problem and Tommy gunned it out of the parking lot.

On the radio, some lady was saying something about shots being fired on Elmore Park Drive.

Tommy drove faster.

2.

Officer Kenneth Wood had been watching the whore for weeks. He'd become fixated on her. He sat in his squad car for hours in the complex's parking lot, watching as she led guy after guy up to her little fuck-nest.

He often thought about going in there and kicking the door down while she was sucking some guy off. Maybe he'd surprise her so much she'd accidentally bite the guy's pathetic little dick in half. The only thing Kenneth couldn't figure out was, what would he do once he kicked the door down? Would he do his job and arrest her — or would he join in on the fun?

If he really wanted her, like he thought he did, then realistically he didn't have to go up there breaking doors down. She was a whore, after all. He could just pay her. Just like all the other guys did. But once she saw the police uniform, she would scramble. Even if he didn't have the uniform on, he was pretty sure she would recognize him from all the times he sat outside the apartment complex in his squad car. No whore would be dumb enough to carry out business with a cop.

And besides, where was the fun in being like every other guy?

Kenneth rubbed his temple. It was getting late. His shift was coming to an end. He dreaded the inevitable discussion with his supervisor about why he'd been patrolling the same street every day this week despite being assigned to different locations. What was he supposed to say? That he had a stupid crush? That he couldn't stalk her during off duty hours lest his wife started getting suspicious?

He looked at the wedding band around his finger. Marge would be expecting him soon. She was making a meatloaf. Friends were coming over. Friends he didn't give a shit about. A wife he didn't give a shit about.

The entrance to the apartment complex

swung open and the whore walked down the stairs and headed across the parking lot. She wiped her mouth like it was still full of someone's sin.

Watching her ass jiggle as she crossed his path, he felt his pants instantly tighten.

He thought about the meatloaf waiting for him at home. He thought about the way Marge would smile when he walked through the door. He thought about how small the whore's top was and how her tits seemed like they were about to burst through the buttons. He thought about vows he had made, both to his wife and to the police force. He thought about bending the whore over the hood of his squad car.

He leaned his head back and closed his eyes, waiting for her to pass. He tried concentrating on anything but her ass. Soon she would be gone and he wouldn't know where she was and he'd be able to return home to his wife.

In his head, Kenneth visualized driving alongside the whore, asking if she needed a ride. But she wouldn't accept his offer. She would tell him to get lost. He would say he was lonely and needed company, and she'd tell him she wasn't born yesterday, that she wasn't gonna work with some dirty fat pig. He would get angry about this, completely fucking outraged, and he'd get out of his squad car and take out his billy club and smack it against her kneecap. Her weight would collapse to the street and he'd beat on her for a bit, bash her pretty face into the pavement. He'd ask her if she wanted to reconsider the ride now.

He'd …

Kenneth opened his eyes. He was no longer in the squad car. He was standing in the middle of the street, breathing hard. His knuckles hurt. He was holding his billy club and he didn't know why.

He looked down. The whore was at his feet, crying, covered in blood, begging for mercy.

"What have I done?" he whispered, then looked around to see if anyone was watching him. He returned the billy club to his belt and picked the whore up in his arms. He stuffed her in the trunk, got back in the car and sped away, his heart pounding hard and his cock throbbing harder.

He wasn't sure what he was doing, but he sure as hell liked it.

But what now?

He couldn't go home with the whore in his trunk. The meatloaf would have to wait. Everything would have to wait. Life had just taken a turn for the better. Everything was changed now. It would never, ever be the same again.

He would need rope. And a shovel. He'd have to erase all evidence afterward.

He was deciding where he would bury her body when he drove into the drugstore parking lot. The thought of her naked corpse sprawled out in the dirt filled him with an inexplicable joy as he locked the car and whistled his way into the store.

He was wondering how loud he'd be able to make her scream when his eyes noticed the man standing at the front counter, holding a gun.

He thought about Marge's meatloaf.

It was going to get very cold.

3.

Nikki was scared.

Tommy was in the bathroom, scrubbing his naked body with a washcloth. His clothes were soaking in the sink. The water had turned dark and dirty from all the blood. So much blood … oh God, where had it come from?

Tommy wasn't injured, so the blood must belong to someone else. The thought of who it could have been made her lightheaded. She had to sit down before she fainted. She dumped the bag of cash on the couch next to her and marveled at all the green.

Tommy walked into the living room, getting dressed. He had a crazy look in his eyes that made her want to get far away from him.

"I did it, sweetheart," he said. "I did it. I got us the money."

"I see that."

"It was hard, but I did it. I did for you. For you and for our new baby."

He rubbed her stomach, smiling like an insane person. She tried scooting away from him as dread swallowed her.

Nikki nodded toward the driveway. "Where'd you get the cop car, Tommy?"

Tommy laughed. Her blood curdled.

"You won't believe this," he said, "but a fuckin' cop walked in on me. *A cop!*"

She didn't want to ask the next question, but she had to. "Tommy, how did you get the cop's *car?*"

"He drew on me. I had to put him down." He smiled again, proud this time. Like he was bragging.

Jesus.

"You shot him? Where the fuck did you get a gun?"

"Uh, Markus gave it to me."

"Your stupid goddamn cousin, Markus?"

"Hey, he's reliable. Don't discredit him."

Nikki paced back and forth. "I thought I told you I didn't want you to have a gun. Jesus Christ, Tommy. You killed a cop? What the fuck is wrong with you?" She wanted to strangle him. How difficult was it to follow one simple direction?

"What did you want me to do, let him arrest me? Christ, Nikki, use some common sense."

"Speaking of common sense," Nikki said, "where's your car? Why'd you take the cop's?"

Tommy laughed. "The fuckin' piece of junk wouldn't start."

"So you left it in the same parking lot where you murdered a cop."

"Yeah."

"Motherfucker, Tommy, mother*fucker*."

"We probably need to go soon. I don't think it's gonna be safe here much longer."

"Oh, you don't think so, huh?" Nikki said. She went into the kitchen for a glass of water. She took her cell phone out of her pocket and texted another message to Eugene: *r u ok???*

So far, he had failed to respond to her last three text messages.

Tommy joined her in the kitchen and got a beer. "I swear to God, baby, I wouldn't have shot them if there had been another way."

He laid a gun on the table. They both stared at it.

"I gotta get rid of this," he said. "Not sure where, though. Maybe the river. What do you think?"

"Wait." Nikki stared at Tommy, then at the gun on the table, then back at Tommy. "Did you just say … *them?*"

"What?"

She grabbed his shoulders and pushed him against the wall. "You said you wouldn't have had to shoot *them. Them* as in plural. As in more than *one.*"

Tommy brushed her hands off him. "I had to get rid of the clerk there too. He witnessed me shoot the fucking cop."

Nikki's lip quivered. "You … you shot him?"

"Whose blood do you think is on my clothes? Christ, honey, this was your idea."

"I told you not to bring a gun. I fucking *told you* to not bring a gun."

"Well, be glad I did. Otherwise I probably wouldn't be here right now."

"Where did you shoot him?"

"The cop?"

"No, the … the other one."

"In the head. I shot him in the head."

Nikki gasped. She surrendered her weight to the kitchen counter to prevent falling on the floor.

"What the hell does it matter?" Tommy asked. "The point is, they're dead and we're not. We did it, baby. We're one step closer."

Nikki grabbed the gun off the table, stuck it in Tommy's face, and squeezed the trigger. Then she did it again. And again.

She dropped the gun on the floor next to his body and pulled her phone back out. She dialed Eugene's number and listened to it ring. It went to his voicemail. She opened her mouth to say something, but no words came out.

She looked back down at Tommy. She told him not to bring a gun. That it would be too dangerous.

Why couldn't he have just listened for once in his miserable life?

She refilled the drugstore bag with the cash, threw it in a duffel bag with some of her belongings, and collected the car keys off the dresser. She got in the cop car parked in her driveway and floored it out of town.

She kept rubbing her belly, thinking how empty it truly was, how Eugene had promised to fill it with a life one day, once they had finally begun their own life together.

Now that would never happen.

She fucking told him no guns.

Her cell phone rang. She didn't recognize the number. She stared at the screen for a few seconds and threw the phone out the window.

Hours passed. Eventually she had to stop and refill the gas tank. She wondered how far she could realistically go with a stolen cop car. She was lucky to even still be on the run, she realized. She needed a different ride. Someone less conspicuous. The cop car was like walking through a sniper's practice field with a bright red target painted on her face.

She parked behind the station's building in an empty field, thinking maybe she could hitch a ride with some horny trucker. She had collected her bags and started to walk away when she heard the noise from the cruiser's trunk.

Thump thump, thump thump, thump thump thump

"What the shit?" she said, approaching the trunk.

She wondered who or what might be inside. Maybe Tommy had hidden Eugene and the cop in there. That would mean one of them was still alive.

Eugene…

Nikki felt a twinge of hope as she popped open the trunk.

4.

Amy had begun to wonder if the car would ever stop. The cop had been driving for hours now. Maybe days. Who knew? Hard to gauge time when you were locked inside a trunk.

Where was this lunatic taking her, anyway?

Someplace deserted, she imagined. Someplace no one could witness him do whatever sick shit he had planned. Well, she wasn't going to let that happen. No fucking way. This wasn't the first time some creep had tried screwing with her.

This time she was ready. She was prepared.

"Never again," she whispered. "Never again."

She had the little snubnose out of her bra and pointed at the trunk door, waiting.

And she wasn't going to lower it until this twisted motherfucker had a few holes in him.

Schmuck

Dennis Day

DOC AND ME ARE out cherry picking when we stop by this station for some gas. It's raining when we pull up to the pump and we hafta wait for the schmuck inside to get off the horn. He waves at us through the glass with a friendly smile, and we consider whether he might have anything in the till worth getting wet for. He finally comes out and I roll down the window and tell him: "Fill-her-up and check the oil." The rain's dropping off the visor of his cap all over me and I tell him to get his fucking head outta my car.

The hood's up and the schmuck's bending over the fender to get a look at the dipstick when this Caddy rolls in on the other side of the island. Schmuck's ass is up in the air where anybody can see he's busy, and what does the Caddy do but honk like maybe nobody sees him sitting there.

Or maybe Caddys're supposed to come first. The guy inside slides across the front seat and gets out in the rain, pulls the collar of his trench coat up around his neck and the brim of his hat down over his eyes. When he sees Doc and me watching him, he pushes the lock button down and slams the door. I look over and Doc's grinning — the best way to get a carjacker's attention is to lock your buggy up.

We swing into action, Doc out his door heading in the station to stall the guy if he tries to come back out before I'm done, and me out mine to see what's inside the Caddy that's worth locking it up. It's pretty dark on the drive and with the rain streaming down the windows it's hard to see inside. Nothing in the front seat except a road map on the dash. Nothing in the back except an old cardboard suitcase on the floor. I try the door handle just in case.

Inside, I find Doc standing with a bottle of pop next to a rack of Firestones. He nods towards the grease room, a dingy *Men's Restroom* sign above the door. I stomp my feet and shake the water off my hat. The pop machine's next to a display of belts and gaskets — I slip in a nickel, slide an orange along the slot and pry off the cap. When I look up, the guy in the Caddy's standing next to the cash register.

This guy's big, a lot bigger than he looked outside, and you can see there ain't no laugh lines on his face. His eyes're dark and he just stands there waiting for Schmuck to get done servicing our car. He glances at me, then turns and looks out the glass at the drive. I take a peep at Doc and he's looking pretty sober. The first thing crosses my mind is this one's a whole lotta trouble. My hunch tells me to leave him alone.

Schmuck comes back in dripping wet and wipes his hands on a grease rag.

"Eight and a half gallons. That'll be ninety-four cents," he says.

I give him a buck and tell him to keep the change.

"Your oil's low," he adds, "when's the last time you had it changed?"

I don't answer. When he opens the till, I see he hasn't made any deposits lately. Doc gives me the nod that says we should hang around.

Then Schmuck turns to the big guy: "What'll it be?"

"Fill it up. Under the hood's fine. Just the gas," the guys says.

Schmuck pulls up his collar and heads back out into the rain. Doc and me stand around drinking our pop and shooting the shit, waiting for the Caddy to drive away. The big guy just stands there, his hands in his coat pockets, staring out at the light reflected on the road while he waits.

"That'll be a dollar seventy-two," Schmuck says when he comes back inside. The guy hands him two Georges and Schmuck pokes three buttons and hits the bar that pops the drawer. Ker-ching. He makes change and says "Nice car. Had it long?" He's grinning when he says it and I wonder what he means.

The big mug don't say a word, just pulls his hat down and heads out the door. I figure we'll wait maybe five minutes and then I'll hold Schmuck up while Doc cleans out the cash register. I drain my pop bottle and I'm looking for the crate to put it in when I hear the door behind me open. Crap, another customer, I say to myself.

But it ain't. It's the big guy back again. And just for a moment, I have this twinge in my gut. He goes up to Schmuck and says: "I'm locked out."

"Keys in the car, huh?" Schmuck says it like he's heard this story a hundred times before. "I got a hangar in the grease room. I'll get it."

"No." The big guy sounds like he's used to giving orders. "That won't work."

"Sure it will," Schmuck says. "I do it all the time."

"Not on this car."

"Ah," says Schmuck, like he's in on something only the two of them know about.

The big guy stands there like a piece of granite, the kind you see in a cemetery. "Phone?" he asks.

"Sure," Schmuck says. "Right there. Reverse the charges if it's long distance."

"A payphone."

Schmuck shakes his head. "Not here. Up the street at the corner drug store they got a booth in the back. But they close in fifteen minutes. You'll hafta hurry."

I see the big guy's thinking about it, leaving the Caddy here while he runs two blocks in the rain, or maybe using Schmuck's horn where all of us can hear every word even without listening.

"Okay," the big guy says. He sits on the stool next to the counter and pulls the phone towards himself. He mumbles something to the operator trying to be quiet, but I hear right away it's a Chicago exchange.

Doc and me look out the window like we ain't interested, but we hear every word.

"Tony?" the big guy says. "Yeah, it's me. You got another set of keys? I locked yours in the car." We can't make out what the guy on the other end is saying, but it's loud and you can tell from the big guy's face he don't like what he's hearing. "Just send Sam out with the other set. I'm at a Texaco station at the intersection of Highway 24 and 117." There's some more static on the other end of the line and then the big guy hangs up without saying goodbye.

I have a hunch. I get a hunch every once in a while when all the pieces in a picture don't fit together just right. And my hunch is telling me this big guy and his big car're worth a helluva lot more to Doc and me than anything we're gonna get outta Schmuck's till.

"Come over here," I say to Schmuck. I look at the name stitched on his uniform. "Okay, Carl. You don't look too busy right now. You think you can handle that oil change? I'll keep my eye on the drive for you and let you know if anyone pulls in."

Schmuck thinks about it for a minute. "I suppose," he says, looking over at the big guy. "I already got one drive blocked anyways. But you'll hafta pull it into the grease room."

Doc slides into the seat next to me as I turn the key. He wants to know what the hell I'm up to.

"The big mug," I tell him. "He locks his Caddy up tight and there's a suitcase behind the driver's seat. Don't want nobody to hear him on the phone neither. I got a feeling in my gut." I guide the front tires into the ramps and up onto the hoist, Schmuck pointing left and then back right. "This guy's hiding something, Doc. And now he's gonna hang around here a couple hours 'til a new set of keys shows up. I'm thinking maybe we oughta get a look inside that suitcase."

"I don't know," Doc says. "You got an idea how to get it done?"

"Maybe. For now, get me another bottle of orange," I say as we climb outta the car.

I watch Schmuck hoist my Model T into the air, roll a cart with a funnel under the oil pan and reach up with his wrench. The plate drops with a clunk and Schmuck reaches for his grease rag.

"W-40 okay?" he asks.

I nod and he carries an oil can over to a barrel and pumps the lever five times. Then he shakes out a cigarette from his deck, lights it and leans against the work bench waiting for the last drop of oil to drip outta the engine.

"How long does it take to get from here to Chicago?" I ask him.

"Depends. Three-and-a-half hours to Midway."

"You get a lot of business on a night like tonight?"

Schmuck looks out at the rain still falling in the darkness beyond the streetlight on the corner. "Nope," he says. "Two cars on the drive at the same time? That ain't happened since I started working here." He picks up a gun attached to the end of a hose and starts pounding shots of grease into nipples below the car's frame.

Doc hands me my second pop. "Where's the big guy?" I ask him.

"Sitting on the pop machine reading a newspaper."

Schmuck reattaches the oil pan, lowers the hoist and pops the hood. We watch him carefully pour the can full of oil into the engine.

"I say we hold both these mugs up at the same time," I tell Doc under my breath. "After we clean out the till, we hangar the door on the Caddy and see what's inside."

"I don't know," Doc says again. "I don't like

the look of that guy. Might be biting off more than we can chew."

"Don't be a baby, Doc," I tease. "Find something we can tie them up with."

When Schmuck's done changing the oil, he comes over and says "That'll be a buck sixty for the oil, ten cents for the grease, and thirty-five cents for the labor."

I see Doc coming up behind him and he's got a coil of clothesline in his hand, so I smile real nice and pull out my rod and poke Schmuck in the gut. "No noise, Carl," I warn him. "Put your hands behind you and back up to that work bench."

Doc wraps Schmuck up with a few rounds of rope and cinches his hands to the vise.

"Okay, Doc," I say, "you go in and tell the big guy you want another pop. When he gets off the machine, I'll come up behind him."

The big guy don't even look at Doc when he asks, like Doc's a bug or something and not worth the trouble. But he gets up and is folding his paper when I poke the barrel of my rod in his back.

"Don't move unless you want one in the kidney," I growl. He freezes like a statue. "Okay, Doc, get the rope."

Doc does to the big guy what he done to Schmuck, only this time he ties him to the pop machine instead. The ape's big enough maybe he can drag it across the floor, but not carry it. "You keep him here while I have a look-see," I say to Doc.

Doc points at the floor with his .38. "Slide on down there and sit cross-leg," he says to the big guy.

I clean out the register while the big guy's getting comfortable. Out in the grease room, I tell Schmuck I need the hangar he uses to unlock cars. It's hanging in the corner next to the overhead door.

Outside on the drive it's still raining, but not as hard. Then I see the joke Schmuck was having, why the big guy said the hangar wouldn't work. I didn't notice before, but this ain't no ordinary Caddy. The windows must be at least an inch thick, and when I bounce on the fender it hardly moves. It's gotta weigh over six tons. I try the hangar anyways, but when I snag the bar, the damned window's so heavy the hangar just bends straight and slips out.

But there's more than one way to skin a cat. I look up and down the highway and there ain't a car in sight. I step back and aim at the middle of the back window. The first shot makes a chip, the second a splinter and the third one shatters the glass into a shower that glitters across the pavement. I reach in and pull the handle to open the door. The suitcase ain't locked, but it has two straps around it. I lay it flat on the floor of the back seat and open the lid. What can I say? Bingo! My hunch is right. The damned thing's full of cash.

I glance down at my watch. It's maybe half an hour since the big guy got off the horn with his guy in Chicago. Even if he got on the road right away, it'll still be two or three hours 'til he gets here with the keys. Plenty of time for me and Doc to lam it.

I'm excited now, but there ain't no time to celebrate yet. I strap the suitcase back together and stash it behind the seat in our car. Then I back out of the grease room and pull back up to the pump outside the front door. I leave the engine running and go inside.

"Okay, Doc," I say, "time to hit the road."

"Do you two idiots know what kinda trouble you're in?" the big guy asks. Most people would look silly sitting on the floor cross-leg with their hands tied behind their back, but the big guy just looks mean. "Come over here," he orders me.

I don't know why I do it, but I step past Doc and look down at him. "Yeah?" I say. "What'ya want?"

"You wanna die, son?" he growls at me. "It ain't too late to put the suitcase back where you found it and get the hell outta here. You do that and maybe you live. You don't and you're dead meat."

"You gotta find us first," I say to him. I sneer to let him know we ain't afraid of him.

"One last thing," I say to Doc. "Find out from Schmuck where the drive lights are."

He does, and as we go out the door, I flip the

switch and the station goes dark like it's closed for the night.

Out on the road I head east a few miles, then take a gravel road south 'til we hit a T, then back west to the highway. Doc flips on the dome light and pulls the suitcase up into his lap.

"Holy shit," he says as he lets the lid of the case lean back against the dashboard. He starts counting the number of bills in a stack and then the number of stacks. "Jesus H. Christ," he says. "There's gotta be fifty grand in here."

I figure it's not too far to St. Louis. We'll hole up there for the night, then head for Tulsa where a guy I know'll put us up 'til this blows over.

We're cruising down the highway in the middle of the night. The rain's stopped, but there's heavy clouds in the sky and the pavement hisses with the sound of our tires. I have my arm out the window and I'm looking at the road where the headlights come together in the dark. But all I'm seeing is those stacks of bills packed inside that suitcase. The air's wet and heavy. It's a perfect night for a drive.

When we get to St. Louis, I keep right on going—I have a hunch. But after a few hours, I can't keep my eyes open no more, and Doc ain't no better. Neither of us can sleep in the car. I see a motel off the side of the road. We pull in, grab three or four hours of sleep and get back on the road.

We're just coming into the outskirts of

Lebanon when I see a red flashing light in my rearview mirror, then hear a siren.

"What the fuck?" Doc says.

"Let me handle this," I say. I pull over to the side of the road and a big sedan pulls in front of me, another behind. "Fucking cops," I say as I reach in my jacket for my license and tuck my rod so it can't be seen.

"Uh, oh," Doc says as five men get out, three on my side and two on his, all of them with guns in their hands.

"Get outta the car, asshole," one of the guys on my side says to me. A second guy pulls open the door and grabs my lapel. He pushes me against the side of the car, pats me down and relieves me of my rod. "Search the car," says the first guy.

"It's here," the second guy says. "You want me to count it?"

"Nah. They ain't had time to spend any yet. Find a phone and let Tony know we got them. He'll tell you where to meet Mike. We'll be in the park south of the pavilion."

They push me and Doc in the backseat of the first sedan, one guy driving and two pointing their rods at us in the back. It ain't far, just around the end of a lake and along a dirt road with picnic tables off to one side. We just sit in the parking lot looking out at the water. There ain't nobody in sight. I ask for a cigarette but the guy says, "Go fuck yourself." Doc says he hasta take a piss and they let him get out for that. By then the sun's starting down, it's afternoon and the air's so wet you can cut it with a knife.

From where I'm sitting in the back seat, I can see the rearview mirror. I recognize my car when it comes around a curve in the road. Following on its bumper is the Caddy. The two guys drag us out and make us kneel next to the shore.

The big man from the gas station gets out of the Caddy and walks over to us. He don't say a word. He just takes out his revolver and shoots Doc in the back of the head.

"Wait a minute," I say, "Just wait a minute."

"What do you want?" he snarls.

"How did you find us?"

"You must think I'm dumb *and* blind," the mug sneers. "Drop-top two-door Model T, Illinois tags 265-065. Guys like you never learn."

The big man moves behind me, his shadow spreading out onto the waves as they lap against the shore. Along the top of the ripples I can see little faint streaks of pink and orange.

"What're you muttering about, schmuck?" the big guy says.

Gods And Virgins In The Big Easy

Nina Mansfield

I CLEARLY REMEMBERED that last shot of *Jagermeister* at The Boot. I somewhat recalled a sloppy game of pool at Miss Mae's. I had a vague recollection of a vomitty kiss at F&Ms. But I had no memory of returning to Burthe Street. I did have a strong feeling I'd done something I shouldn't have, but I sure as hell didn't remember killing anyone.

Of course, murder *had* been the purpose for our road trip. Nashville to New Orleans and back. Arti said no one would miss us. No one would know. She had it all planned out. I didn't think she was serious, though. Not really.

But there it was, that keepsake Swiss Army knife. Neon green, blade out. "Big Easy" written in block letters. Lying on a pile of my clothes, which were damp from a leak in the ceiling, and mixed with Mardi Gras beads and mud. There was a reddish-brown streak smeared across the T-shirt I'd bought the day before in the French Quarter. A souvenir from my first college road trip.

"Better pay in cash, Callisto," Arti said. Most people called me Callie, but Arti always insisted on using my full name.

I played along. "I get it. So our whereabouts this weekend can't be traced."

Pretending to plan a murder was just the sort of thing best friends did, wasn't it? It was all make-believe, or at least that's what I kept telling myself. Besides, I didn't need my parents seeing charges from New Orleans on the "food and emergencies only" credit card they'd given me for my freshman year at Vanderbilt.

Arti pocketed the knife while I paid for the shirt. "It's pretty much untraceable, but better safe than sorry," she told me as we made our way down the booze-soaked street afterward.

Our streetcar ride downtown Saturday morning had been incognito. Arti had pushed her white-blonde hair into a ponytail under an LSU baseball cap. I wore dark sunglasses and a kerchief. Arti wasn't really into sightseeing, but I managed to convince her.

"Look, if I am going down to New Orleans with you so that you can stick a knife in your 'cheatin' man's heart,'" I did a poor imitation of

Arti's southern drawl, "then, at the very least, I'd like to visit the French Quarter. Maybe eat a beignet. Drink a hurricane."

I was only three weeks into my freshman year. I was pretty sure that being involved in a murder would make me lose my scholarship. Only seventeen. A Long Island Girl. I figured going to college in the South would sort of be like going to a different country.

Arti was from a different universe.

I'd met her the first week of school. She'd been riding the bull at Gilley's. I mean the one in Nashville. Tight jeans and checkered top, hair waiving like some welcome flag. All legs and elbows. Skinny and round in all the right places, which made me feel shorter and squatter than usual. When she flew off the bull she landed like a butterfly.

"You lasted longer than anyone else," I told her when I ran into her in the bathroom. I rarely talked to strangers. Southern hospitality wasn't my thing, but something about Arti seemed worth the effort.

"I'm glad someone was watching." She winked at me, smoothed back her hair, and asked if I had any red lipstick. I didn't.

"Oh darlin', red is your color," she said. "Brunette like you." She reached down and brushed a strand of hair out of my eyes. For a moment I thought she might kiss me.

She was right about the lipstick. These days I

wear it all the time. Arti seemed to be alone, and the girl from my dorm who had dragged me to Gilley's was busy making out with some guy in the corner, so we bought a pitcher of Natty Light. Drinking age in Nashville was twenty-one, but my bad fake ID—Massachusetts misspelled—seemed to do the trick.

Arti was a sophomore transfer student from LSU, and nothing like the other girls I'd met at school so far. More ripped jeans than pearls. More pool hall than sorority house.

"So, what brings a Yankee like you down South?" she asked. Her lips moved slowly, her perfect teeth shined. "You runnin' away from somethin'?"

"Scholarship," I answered, which was only half true. I didn't want to drag up all my high school baggage—how my best friend stole my boyfriend senior year—how I wanted to go to school where no one would know me—how I basically hated my life.

"I'm gonna be a country music star someday," she said. "Figured Nashville was the place to be. Funny thing about it is, I can't sing for shit." She downed her beer and poured another. I tried to keep up.

Before long I was telling her everything.

"Some friends will stab you in the back the second you turn around," she said.

"But you would only stab them in the front." I laughed at my own joke.

"You got that right."

We were on our second pitcher and I was slurring my words. And right then and there, I decided if Arti would be my friend, I would do anything for her.

The night I met Arti was the first time I ever blacked out drunk.

That Saturday night in New Orleans was the second.

We'd been hanging out in my room when Arti suggested the road trip. She'd become a permanent fixture in my life since that night at Gilley's. She made me forget I needed to keep a 3.0 average for my scholarship. That I actually needed to attend class to do that. She made me forget my entire senior year of high school had ever happened.

On the nights we weren't playing pool upstairs at Gold Rush, or catching a band at Exit/In, we were sneaking cigarettes out the window of my dorm room and watching *Melrose Place*. I had a single on the fourth floor of Dyer Hall—the Virgin Vault—the one dorm floor on the Vanderbilt campus that prohibited males at all times. Some girls got stuck there because their parents were old-school strict, but I'd just screwed up my housing forms. I remember checking the form off for a single. The virgin thing must have been subconscious.

"Brice stopped returning my calls, and he has not responded to any of my letters," Arti said on one of those nights, letting a puff of smoke out into my room. I fanned it out the window with a *Cosmo*. "That sweet-talking son-of-a-bitch, I am gonna kill him."

"Your boyfriend?" I asked, for clarification. In all honesty, I had thought Arti was making him up. She said they'd grown up together in Lafayette, and that he looked like a Greek god. Tall, blonde, pre-med at Tulane. A guy like that, if he existed, might make me reconsider the vow of celibacy I'd taken when I found my ex-best friend straddling my boyfriend in the back seat of my mint-green Tercel.

"He's back with Daphne. I know he is," Arti rambled on. I'd heard the story at least twelve times by then. Brice, the love of her life, blah, blah, blah—the slutty sorority chick who stole him away. According to her, this Daphne chick was the epitome of evil, but worse because she didn't look the part. "She's just *too* cute," Arti said. "Never trust the cute ones."

I guessed that meant I wasn't. Whenever Arti mentioned Daphne's name, her face contorted into pure hatred. It was her second favorite topic, right after "the evils of sorority rush."

"It's only a seven-hour drive to The Big Easy," Arti said. "If we leave early Friday morning—"

"What about class?" I interrupted.

She shrugged. "You got a test or somethin'?"

"No."

"I'ma drive down Friday and come back Sunday. Maybe Monday. Soon as I get this Brice situation settled. I'm fixin' to lose my mind setting here thinking about it nonstop."

"And you need me to come with you?" I asked.

She nodded, took another drag from her cigarette. "For moral support. Plus, I'll need someone to help me dispose of the body."

Arti drove a cream-colored sedan that smelled like Pine Sol and sex and did not at all suit her personality. There were gummy bears stuck between the seats, though I'd never seen her eat a gummy bear. She drove while I slept, and around four o'clock that Friday afternoon we pulled up in front of an old shotgun house, the kind I always pictured when I thought of the South. Lemonade on the front porch and women fanning themselves and all that. Except there was a window boarded up on the second floor and the white paint had all but chipped off.

"Brice shares this place with some guy who practically died from alcohol poisoning the first week of school, so he has the place to himself."

"And what? Are you gonna just knock on the door, pull out a gun, and shoot him?" I said.

"Don't be ridiculous," Arti replied. "My guns are all at home. Besides, I want to make sure my suspicions are correct first. It would be a *sin* to kill an innocent man."

I rolled down the car window and waited

while she went to the door. The air felt like Florida and smelled like barbecue.

After a moment, Arti returned to the car. "Looks like no one's home."

"So what do we do?"

"We wait, see if Brice makes an appearance," Arti said, showing me the key she'd found under the doormat. And with that, in we went.

There was a couch that looked like it had been puked on at least five times, and a squeaky ceiling fan circling overhead. I swore I saw a rat scurry by. One room lead into the other, shotgun style — living room, kitchen and two bedrooms in back. Arti immediately started searching Brice's bedroom for evidence of his infidelity. He was a slob, so it didn't make much of a difference when she emptied his drawers onto the floor. She kept muttering Daphne's name like she expected to find her stashed under the mattress. Only thing she found there was a well-used copy of *Hustler*.

"My letters aren't here," Arti said when she finished searching his room. I've written him at least five since school started. If he still loved me, he would have kept my letters."

There was cold beer in the fridge, which was a good thing, because Arti said I shouldn't drink the water, and the window units barely made a dent in the heavy hot air.

We sat, we drank. Arti found a half-smoked joint in an ashtray that we finished off.

When Brice didn't come home, I crashed on

the mattress and box spring in the back room that belonged to the absent roommate. It had either been there or the puke couch. I should have picked the couch, as it turned out. There was this crazy rain storm in the wee hours, and the roof leaked onto the bed as I slept.

I woke up to the sounds of rain and sex. This was unfortunate, since my bladder was quite full, and there was no way I was going to walk through Brice's bedroom to get to the bathroom. The drip, drip, drip from the ceiling didn't help, but somehow I managed not to wet myself. By the time I decided it was safe to leave the room, Arti was already up making breakfast, and Brice was gone.

"Mornin' sunshine." Arti smiled. She was wearing boxers and a ripped T-shirt that hung off her shoulders.

"Someone looks happy."

She smiled, all post-coital glow. "I'm cookin' grits. Want some?"

"I guess Brice made it home last night?"

"He sure did," she answered.

"Where'd he go?" I looked around like he might be hiding in a corner.

"Says he's got fraternity business all weekend."

I found it sort of ironic that Arti would speak so ill of sorority girls, but have no problem spreading her legs for a frat boy.

"So I guess your plans to kill him are off?" I

asked, teasing.

"Of course not. I was just confirming my suspicions. He still smelled like slutty sorority girl. That was just my way of saying goodbye. I mean, a girl does have her needs."

Arti had changed her mind somewhat about how to kill Brice. "I was gonna do it here, chop up his body in the bathtub or somethin'. But I've reconsidered."

"Oh, that's good." I shoveled some grits into my mouth.

"We gotta make it look more random."

"We?"

"That's what best friends are for, darlin'." She wiped some grits off my chin.

Her new plan involved making Brice's death look like a mugging, or some drunken bar incident. When I realized we had the whole day to kill—no pun intended—I suggested a little sightseeing. Bourbon Street and Café du Monde.

"If you must." Arti rolled her eyes. "At least we won't be in danger of running into anyone I know there."

She whispered her strategy to me at the Acme Oyster House over seafood gumbo and `etoufee. "We just need to figure out where he's gonna be at tonight—catch him while he's alone. You'll distract him, and I'll …" She made a slicing motion with her hand.

"And how, exactly, am I going to 'distract him'?" I asked.

"You're prettier than you think Callisto. On the sturdy side, but pretty."

I wasn't sure if I should thank her or feel insulted.

"Once we get him where we want him, I use this little thing here to slice his carotid." She waved the neon-green knife in front of my nose. "He'll have been drinking. That always makes the blood flow faster."

"So, just to clarify, no guns?"

"Bullets can be traced."

"And if someone sees us?"

"We'll be incognito, darlin'. Besides, no one will be sober enough to remember."

"Sounds like a plan," I said, and ordered another Abita.

Saturday afternoon became a blur after that. Hurricanes at Pat O'Brien's, a walk through Jackson Square. It was dark outside when Arti shook me awake from my day-drinking induced nap with my clothes stuck to my body and the sweat smelling like metabolizing alcohol. I had passed out on that puked-on couch. Arti was belting something off-key and country while mopping up the floor.

"What all have you touched?" She asked once she saw I was awake.

"Sorry?"

"With your greasy little paws?"

I was still perplexed.

"Fingerprints, stupid."

I shrugged. "I don't know. Bathroom. Fridge. That backroom."

Arti shook her head like I was useless. I headed for the shower. "I already cleaned the bathroom, so just wipe down anything you touch," she ordered. For the first time that weekend, I thought she was actually serious about killing Brice—that it wasn't just some twisted game we were playing.

I drank a beer in the shower. When I came out, Arti was incognito again. She tossed me a hat.

"You'll just look like a jackass with sunglasses at night," she said.

You'd think it would've cooled down, just a little. Maybe it's just that everywhere we went was so crowded, bodies pressed up against each other, but the night seemed hotter than the day.

We hopped from bar to bar. Arti would scope it out. If there was no Brice inside, we didn't stay long.

There was crawfish and beer and shots of *Jager* interspersed throughout. Conversations where I couldn't hear a word and cigarettes bummed from strangers. Mud covered my sandaled feet, and little wisps of hair stuck to the back of my neck. At some point, I lost track of Arti. I tried to find her, I really did. But she didn't stand out like she normally did with her hair all tucked up in a cap. And it's not like I could go around asking for her.

"We need to stay invisible," she'd said. "We

need to blend in."

The floor at F&Ms must have had three inches of sludge on it, and after puking for the second time that night, I wiped out leaving the bathroom. As I sat with my ass in the sludge starting to feel sorry for myself at having lost Arti, someone reached down and pulled me up. I hoped to God it was Arti, but it wasn't.

"Want to dance?" the tall guy asked. He was no Adonis, but he didn't seem to mind the sludge on my ass.

"I need to find my friend," I replied. My eyes searched the wall of people that surrounded us for Arti.

"What?" he yelled, and then he said something that I couldn't make out because the music was so loud.

"I said I need to … never mind." I didn't see Arti, and there was nowhere else to go. Someone spilled a beer down my back but I was too drunk and filthy to care anymore. It felt cool, actually, so I started to dance. The guy slipped his hands into the back pockets of my jean shorts and kissed me as we moved.

That was the last thing I remembered until I woke up on the puke couch next morning covered in blood.

What the hell happened? How the hell did I get here?

I felt like I'd been run over by a streetcar, like someone had crushed glass into my eyeballs. A dry heave sent pain throughout my entire body. I thought all my insides would come out.

"Arti? Are you here?" I tried to call out as loud as I could, but the muscles in my abdomen prevented me from making much noise.

And that's when I noticed that the blood wasn't just on my hands. It was leaking from my side.

"Holy shit! Arti! Arti!" All that blood, it was mine.

"Arti!"

She pounced from somewhere, lioness out for the kill. "I thought you were dead!" The Swiss Army knife was back in her hand. I thrashed, I kicked, but Arti was unstoppable.

"I said distract him, not screw him, you Yankee bitch!" she screamed.

What the hell? I was sure my entrails would come spilling out at any moment.

They say when you are about to die, your entire life flashes before your eyes. There were only two images that popped into my mind while I struggled to escape Arti's wrath. The first was of my high school best friend mounted on top of my boyfriend in the back of my Tercel. The second was of Arti, riding the bull at Gilley's.

She might have killed me too, except out of nowhere appeared this dark-haired, green-eyed angel — all sundress and apple pie. "Arti, what the fuck!" she exclaimed, her voice simultaneously sharp and sweet.

Arti dropped the knife. "Daphne!"

So, that's Daphne, I thought. She looked like a cuter version of me.

"Brice, what's goin' on?" Daphne demanded.

"Yeah, Brice, what's goin' on?" Arti echoed.

"Yes, Brice, what is going on?" I figured I would join in the fun.

"Aww shit!" Brice stood shirtless, in boxers, in the doorway to his room. His lip twitched into a half-smile as he looked at Arti, then Daphne, then me. "Listen, Daphne, Arti, um, whatever your name is, I can explain."

Daphne didn't wait around for explanations. But her appearance made Arti forget about killing me.

It struck me then. *Oh, so that's Brice*. He looked better that morning than he had the previous night, when he'd scooped me off the floor at F&Ms. But Greek god? That was a bit of a stretch.

Arti lunged for him, but he held down her arms and whispered something in her ear. Next thing I knew, they were making out.

"Um, guys? A little help." Nausea overcame me. I vomited on the couch, and then I passed out.

When I came to, Brice was pouring vodka on my stab wound. I must have screamed, because he slapped his hand over my mouth.

"No need to make a fuss. Looks like it's just a flesh wound," he said, and taped some gauze on it.

Arti sat by his side, looking concerned. "Darlin' I thought I killed you."

She stroked my face. I smacked her hand. "You are fucking crazy!"

Arti actually looked insulted. "Crazy how? 'Cause I didn't walk away from a situation that should be stopped? Seriously, what did you expect me to do when I came home and found you all indecent on the couch with Brice?"

Arti had turned it all around. She might have tried to kill me, but I was definitely the bad guy.

"Look, sugar." She squeezed my hand, all maternal. "I know you've felt this way before."

Arti was right. But I hadn't stabbed anyone.

"Now, you're the second best friend I've caught with my man," Arti continued. "I'd be a fool if I didn't try to kill you."

"Daphne was your best friend?" She'd never mentioned that part. So, Arti and I weren't that different after all.

"Pledge sister too," Brice added and Arti shot him a look like he'd just exposed her darkest secret.

"Sweetie, you know you only try to kill the ones you really love."

Maybe she was right. Maybe she was wrong. But I would travel back to Nashville by bus. I'd make it back to campus just in time to register for sorority rush. And I'd put in for a room transfer. Wasn't quite sure I belonged in the Virgin Vault anymore. Then again, I was a bit cloudy about the details on what exactly had happened with Brice. Arti could've helped me fill in the gaps, but I never spoke to her again. I decided I'd rather have friends that stab you in the back then stab you in the front. Both might hurt, but I preferred the method with less blood.

Slit The Belly

S. A. Cosby

TRON BANGED ON THE OLD screen door so
hard the whole house seemed to shake. Day-Day
heard shuffling footsteps approach the door. He
reflexively touched the butt of the Glock in his
waistband rubbing against the small of his back.
A robin whistled from a nearby magnolia tree.
What sounded like a pretty good-sized dog
barked in the distance.

An old man with skin as black as midnight in
a mineshaft opened the door. "Can I help you
boys?" he said.

"We looking for Trucky," Tron said in a deep
voice. It reminded Day-Day of Darth Vader.

"He ain't here. He went to the store but
should be back presently. You fellas wanna come
in and wait for him?" the old man asked.

"Yeah. We can do that," Tron said. The old

man smiled and walked back into his kitchen. Tron and Day-Day followed him. The old man sat down at circular metal table. Day-Day and Tron sat across from him. A steaming cup of coffee sat in front of the old man.

"I'm Alvin Lee, Trucky's grandfather," the old man said, holding out his hand. "What they call you boys?"

Tron looked at the hand then back at the old man's face.

"I'm Tyrone and this is Duane," Tron said. Legally that was true. Those were their given names. No one in the street would even flinch at those names. But tell them Tron and Day-Day were coming and homeboys suddenly found religion. Alvin pulled his hand back and took a sip of his coffee.

"Trucky got so many friends it's hard to keep track. They coming by all times of the day and night. He's always had a lot of friends. I think it's his way of dealing with his parents dying. My daughter and son-in-law was killed in a car accident. We took Trucky in after. Then his grandmother passed. Lost my little girl and my wife in the same year," Alvin said.

"Damn," Day-Day said. He'd killed four people in his life but never wiped out a whole family.

Alvin nodded as if he understood. Tron looked over the old man's shoulder at the rooster clock on the wall.

"How long Trucky been gone?" Tron said. Alvin answered his question with a question.

"How you boys know Trucky?"

Tron smirked. It looked like a snarl to Day-Day. "We just know him," he said.

Alvin smiled. "I know how that is. I ain't so old I don't remember what it's like to have running partners. Believe it or not I used to roll with some rough boys back in the day. Some real Nicky Barnes and Frank Lucas type of brothers. "For real?" Day-Day said. Tron shot him a look. Alvin nodded his head.

"Yes sir. And before me my daddy was a rum runner for a fella out of Franklin County. Carried moonshine up the Potomac to the juke joints. Trucky, though, he ain't about that kind of life. He always been nice, you know? He not cut out to slit no bellies," Alvin said.

"Huh?" Day-Day said.

Alvin laughed. He laughed long and hard. The skin on Day-Day's neck pimpled with gooseflesh.

"My daddy told me if things got out of hand on the boat or one of them Northerners come up short, sometimes you had to dump them overboard. But you slit they belly first and poke holes in they lungs so they don't float back to the surface." Alvin smiled again.

"Damn, man. That's messed up," Day-Day said.

Alvin laughed again, softly this time. "Yeah,

I guess it is. But you do messed up things and messed up things might happen to you, too," he said.

"What Trucky go to the store for?" Tron said.

Alvin's hard, brown eyes studied Tron.

"He said he had to get some things," Alvin said after a moment.

"Like what?" Tron asked.

"I don't know. Things," Alvin said.

"What store he go to? We passed a 7-11 on our way here and ain't seen him," Tron said.

Day-Day sighed. It was about to go down. He was actually sort of enjoying the old man's stories.

Alvin sipped his coffee and set it down, then put his hands flat on the table.

"Ya know when he told me you boys was coming I thought ya'll would be some real hard rocks. But ya'll just some wanna be gangsters. Baby shit soft," Alvin said.

Tron cocked his head to the side and stared at the old man.

No one said anything for a few moments. Day-Day could hear the clock on the wall ticking in the silence. He decided fuck it, reached for his Glock.

Alvin's hand went under the table.

A muzzle flash lit up the underside of the table like a fireworks display. Day-Day felt something hot punch him in the guts. He slid out of his chair and onto the floor, blood pouring down his thighs and soaking into his jeans. Tron shoved himself backwards from the table as Alvin stood up holding a sawed-off shotgun, pumped the action and fired a second round into Tron's face, which evaporated as his body collapsed to the floor. A thin ribbon of smoke unfurled from the shortened barrel as Alvin walked around the table and casually aimed it at Day-Day's head.

"Me? I ain't got no heart," Alvin continued. "I did twelve years in Mecklenburg. My heart is gone. And now my grandson gone, too. He was so scared of you boys he hung himself this morning in the shed out back."

Alvin pumped the action on the shotgun and expelled a still smoking shell. It clattered to the floor by Day-Day's head with a dry, hollow sound. Day-Day heard someone gurgling and realized it was him.

Alvin smiled once more. "Lucky for me there's an old outhouse in the woods, so ain't gonna have to slit either of you open, just throw you down the shit hole where you belong." He pulled the trigger. Just before the pellets entered his brain Day-Day tried to speak. He tried to say he was sorry. But the only thing that came out of his mouth was blood.

Hipster Pantsin'

Travis Richardson

"GOT ONE. TWO O'CLOCK, leavin' the parkin' lot," Rick said, looking through his binoculars.

George squinted through his pair. "I see 'im."

"Is this the one?" Rick added.

George furrowed his brow and nodded. "Yep, he'll be the tiebreaker. Let's do this, Cuz."

"Hell yeah," Rick said. "Let me get in position first before you go."

He clambered out of the passenger seat and into the back of the van, kicking empty beer cans in his wake. A wicked grin crossed George's mouth as he stomped on the gas, causing Rick to tip over. Rick shouted profanities at his cousin. George slammed on the brakes four seconds later and Rick rolled up to the front.

"Get 'em, Cuz. Get 'em," George said.

"Stop doin' that, dumbass," Rick replied. He

crawled over to the cargo van's sliding door and jerked it open.

In front of him stood an open-mouthed, bearded twenty-something with a man bun, frozen in shock after nearly being squashed by the out of control van.

"Come on in, hipster," Rick said, grabbing the skinny man's arm and yanking him into the darkness.

"Hey …"

George was on top of him a second later, a Maglite beam blinding his eyes. The hipster threw his hands up to block the light. That's when Rick pulled on the guy's low cut, tight pants.

"Dammit all, I hate these nut-huggers."

"Help!" The man cried.

"Best you shut it or you'll get the business end of this flashlight," George said.

Rick finally tugged the jeans to the man's knees, and then pulled his mustache-printed boxers down.

"Please don't rape me," the hipster whispered.

George shone the light on the man's genitals. His eager face crumbled in disappointment. "Ah, you're fuckin' kiddin' me," he said.

Rick let out a yelp with his arms raised. "Victory is mine, bitch!"

The hipster looked back and forth at his jackass abductors, confused.

"Get the fuck outta my van," George said,

glaring at his hostage, "or I'll beat the livin' shit outta ya."

The hipster shoved himself up and out the door, his pants still puddled around his ankles. He took a few steps before he tripped and landed with his bare ass pointed up into the night sky.

Rick howled with laughter. "Thanks a bunch, hipster," he said.

George yelled, "Fuckin' asshole," as he slid the door closed.

"You're just a sore loser."

"Fuck you."

George dropped behind the wheel and shifted into drive. They sped down July Alley toward Crowdust Street in Deep Ellum. That's when a Dallas PD cruiser pulled in front of them, lights flashing blue and red, blocking their path. George hit the brakes, causing Rick to smash his face against the dashboard.

"Son of a bitch," Rick said as blood flowed from his nose and through his fingers.

George shifted the van into reverse, obliterating the driver's side mirror along a metal fence and scraping the paint off a couple of cars and a Dumpster. The flashing lights and whooping siren from the police cruiser behind the van didn't faze George as his foot remained on the accelerator. He smashed into the cruiser and kept moving backwards. Officers ran into the alley, service weapons raised.

"I don't think we're getting' out of this," Rick

said.

"Not if I can help it," George replied through gritted teeth.

Smoke and burnt rubber filled the air as the van's wheels spun, slowly pushing the DPD cruiser back.

"Fuck this. I'm outta here," Rick said, opening up the door. "You still owe me fifty." He only made it a few feet before he was swarmed by cops and thrown to the ground. The driver's door flew open and an enormous bodybuilding cop jerked George out of his seat, slamming him face first into the side of the van.

"Dude, we're on the same side," George spat with a mouth full of blood.

"You're only on the side of my fist," the officer said.

George tried to push off the filthy van and take a swing at the officer but met 50,000 volts of electricity instead.

***

The arraignment hearing was set for the next morning. George and Rick were bandaged up and decked out in prison uniforms. They waited in a small room, cuffed to a table. An overweight, pasty-faced defense lawyer with a high-pitched drawl walked into the room. George mouthed the word "gay" and Rick nodded, rolling his eyes.

The lawyer, Karl, explained to them that if they pled guilty to three counts of kidnapping and aggravated assault, the DA would be willing to overlook two of the other victims, as well as the resisting arrest and destruction of police property charges.

"It's a great deal and I recommend you should take it," he said.

"How many years we lookin' at?" George asked.

"Probably ten to forty for each count, so thirty to one hundred and twenty years."

Rick and George looked at each other, eyes bugged and mouths wide.

"Bullshit to that," Rick said, his voice an octave higher from his bandaged, broken nose.

"This is ridiculous," George said. "We was just havin' some fun. We didn't kill or rape no one."

Karl pushed up his wire glasses, his sweaty hand trembling. "If you did either of those crimes, it might be easier to defend. Regardless, you two can't beat these charges. You've got five victims and a dozen police officers who will testify against you. You'll get life without parole if you fight."

"But a hundred-year sentence isn't life? Gimme a break, man," Rick said.

"We're fightin' this. With or without your queer ass," George said.

Karl reddened.

"What my cousin is sayin' is that we're not pleadin' guilty," Rick said.

Karl sighed. "Okay, then."

Their lawyer went on to tell them how they should sit still and answer the judge whenever he asked them questions. Neither of the cousins paid much heed, both still livid about the charges.

"This is the biggest steaming pile of BS I've seen," Rick said.

"We only messed around with faggoty-ass liberal hipsters. Nobody gives a damn about them."

"Don't say anything like that to the judge," Karl said. He tried to give them a stern look, but it came off like he was constipated instead. "The less attention you bring to yourselves, the lower the bail will be. So keep your opinions to yourself, do both of you understand me?"

"Sure, counselor," George said, scratching his chin with his middle finger.

***

An hour later they stood before the judge with Karl. George noticed a couple of buddies in the courtroom and nodded to them. The prosecutor was a blonde woman with a stern demeanor. She listed all of the crimes the two had committed on their hipster pantsin' escapade.

"Uptight bitch," George whispered.

"No doubt," Rick answered.

Karl hushed them.

The judge, a heavy, balding man, shook his head after hearing the charges. "Before I ask each of you how you'd plead, I want to ask what was going through your minds to do what you did?"

Karl objected, but the judge said he was talking to the boys. "They don't have to answer, but I'd still like to know."

"I don't mind," Rick said. "It was a bet, Your Honor. And George here owes me fifty dollars."

"You're tellin' me you two caused all this mayhem and destruction over a fifty-dollar bet?"

"Sir, my clients were misguided and, uh …" Karl stammered. "They didn't mean to harm anybody. Just pulling a prank."

"And what did this bet hinge on?"

"Your Honor …"

"I want to hear it from the accused. You boys can talk."

George spoke up. "Me and Rick, we just wondered if hipsters shaved their balls or not."

The courtroom laughed. The judge did a full-on spit take from his coffee mug. He grabbed a handful of tissues to wipe his chin and the bench.

"Excuse me?"

"You see, these hipster types in Deep Ellum," Rick said. "They grow long scraggly beards and tie their hair into buns, but we had a feeling most of 'em was also manscapin'. Kind of a contradiction if you asked me."

"Manscaping?"

"Shavin' their nutsacks, chest, stuff like that. We was just curious and didn't mean to hurt nobody."

"Not too bad, anyway," George whispered a

little too loud.

"Your Honor," Karl began.

"I wanna hear from them, not you," the judge said, pointing a stern finger at the lawyer. He turned back to the boys. "So what did you find out?"

"Three of 'em did, two didn't," Rick said with a triumphant smile.

"You just got lucky," George said.

The judge chortled. "Good Lord. So how do you two plead?"

"Not guilty," they both answered.

"Of course. I'll set bail at three hundred thousand each with a court date on November eighth."

The judge banged that gavel and called the next case. Both cousins turned toward Karl, their faces drained of blood.

"What the hell was that? We don't have that kind of money," George said.

Deputies grabbed both of them, leading them back to the holding pen.

"See you two in a couple of months," Karl said, stuffing papers into a briefcase.

"Don't worry, guys," a friend shouted while another took pictures with his phone. "We'll let people know what happened."

***

While the boys sat in a detaining cell, their

hipster-pantsing incident was already blowing up in the media, from both legitimate and fake news sources. Local news covered the event like the cousins had masterminded a three-hour reign of terror, interviewing a couple of the victims and several witnesses. Alt-right bloggers took the approach that the two were having harmless fun and the liberal, politically-correct media was blowing the entire situation out of proportion.

By the time George and Rick, cuffed in chains, unloaded from a bus at the Hutchins penitentiary, their antics had inspired a national upheaval. Not that they knew anything about it. They trembled so bad that their teeth chattered after receiving multiple threats of sodomy and other forms of suffering in English as well as Spanish. It was impossible to look tough around hardcore criminals. The cousins knew they stood out like the fresh meat they were.

"Holy shit, this sucks," George said.

"It was your idea."

"Well you were the dumbass who took me up on the offer. That makes you twice as stupid as me."

George shoulder-shoved Rick. Rick rammed him with his head, knocking George on his ass, which caused Rick to fall on top of his cousin since their chains were tethered.

The prisoners cheered as the two scuffled. A deputy sprayed a can of mace point-blank in their faces.

Fire seared both of the cousins' lungs as they tried to scrape away the pain searing their eyeballs. Four guards rushed out and separated them from the group, giving each a few blasts from their Tasers for good measure.

"Let's process these idiots separately," a head guard said as his comrades tugged the limp cousins inside.

***

"What happened to good ol' fashioned American fun? Free the Hipster Pantsers," a prominent men's rights advocate posted on Twitter, with a link to a blog of the incident portraying the cousins as victims that night. By morning, fake news sites across the nation were speculating that the prosecutor ran a child prostitution ring and the judge secretly sacrificed babies to a satanic cult. Even mainstream conservative commentators weighed in on the issue, saying that anything more than a year in jail was a miscarriage of justice. "We all make mistakes sometimes," was a reoccurring phrase they used. They dismissed the destruction of police property as something the Dallas PD started.

***

When George and Rick were led out of confinement into the main yard, they walked as fast as they could to each other like magnets. They kept their heads down, lest they make eye contact with somebody who wanted to follow through with their threat.

"Cuz," George said.

"Cuz," Rick repeated.

"Got my back?"

"Of course, dipshit. You better have mine."

"No doubt." George spat and kicked the ground. "You get the feelin' that everybody's watchin' us?"

Rick nodded, goosebumps rising on his arms. "I do."

"I'd rather die than get my bumhole raped by these fuckers."

"Me too."

"We'll go down fightin'."

"Yep."

George looked up for a quick moment, and glanced around the yard.

"I'll be damned."

"Dude, put your head back down," Rick said.

"No, man. Look up."

Rick knew better than to listen to his cousin, but curiosity got the better of him.

"What the …"

Men in the yard were looking at them, but instead of glaring at them with hostility, they nodded at them with respect. Blacks, whites, Latinos, all of them. What the hell?

***

At about the time that George and Rick were getting acquainted with their fellow inmates, a hacker published the pantsing victims' names and contact information online. Immediately, death threats from all over the country went to them. By the end of the day three accusers had dropped their charges against the cousins. A Go Fund Me page to raise bail money for the pantsers hit $200,000 in the first hour.

***

Larry "Pudge" Paxton was a guard in the yard that nobody respected. Soft in the belly and the head, he tried to act like a badass, but nobody bought it. Rick walked up to him. Pudge's eyes lit up.

"What's up, fish? Make any friends yet?"

"I, uh, wondered if you might have any pointers about that," Rick said.

Pudge scratched his chin like a wise sage considering how best to impart advice on a young prisoner. "Well, my first advice is to cover your butt. Especially in the showers. You see …"

Pudge's words were cut short as Rick pushed him in the chest, hard. Pudge fell backwards over George, who had snuck up behind him on hands and knees. Pudge hit the ground with an umph. A cloud of dust rose in his wake. Before Pudge could figure out what had happened, his belt was loosened and pants yanked down past his knees.

"Don't rape me," he screamed, his eyes

squeezed shut.

"All natural," George said, ignoring him.

"Figures," Rick said.

Pudge heard shouts and groans, but no shots from the tower. He opened one eye and saw a gaggle of smirking prisoners glancing from his face to his exposed privates.

"Come on, man, pull up yer shorts," a familiar voice said.

Pudge looked over at Big Tex, an enormous guard with wide shoulders not unlike the cowboy statue at the Texas State Fair. He had a cruel smile and everyone, inmates and colleagues, steered clear of him.

"I … I was just assaulted," Pudge said to Big Tex.

"Naw, them boys was just havin' some fun. Now pull up yer panties and act like a man."

Pudge blinked, not understanding at first. Big Tex clapped his meaty paws together like thunder. "Come on, you're embarrassin' yourself, Pudgy. Pull 'em up."

While the portly correctional officer scrambled to pull his pants up, he heard snickers from the nearby inmates. Good Lord, he'd never be able to stare any of them down anymore, would never be able to wield authority in the yard again. He ran out of the yard before they saw tears welling up in his eyes. He needed a new job, starting right now.

***

Across the nation, schools and police reported a spike in pantsing incidents. In less than two days it became an epidemic. Common victims were trendy men with beards and man buns. A legislator in Oklahoma wrote a bill that would ensure that pantsing incidents would be treated as a misdemeanor rather than assault. The president tweeted that he might pants some prominent House members if they didn't pass his controversial tax provision, and it was re-tweeted nearly one million times.

***

A week after the incident, the cousins received their bail money with a surplus. They stood outside the Dallas Municipal Courthouse to a crowd of several hundred amped-up men and the media. Metallica's "And Justice For All" played over loudspeakers.

"Holy shit," Rick said.

A sideways smile cracked on George's face. "Looks like we're heroes or somethin'."

Karl stood behind them, nervously wiping sweat off his forehead. He'd instructed them to not say anything that could be used against them since the trial was technically still scheduled to happen. A squat, blond man who ran a famous alt-right website introduced the cousins. He likened the cousins to American revolutionaries.

"These boys are shakin' things up, much like the founders did with that wild and raucous tea party a few years back," he said.

Cheers went up and the cousins stepped up to the podium. The crowd silenced, waiting for George and Rick to say a few words.

"Wow, it's an honor to be with y'all today," Rick said.

"This has been a … long and, ah … hard journey … we have been tested … as men. And we stood up. You have no idea." George shook with conviction.

Men in the audience nodded their heads.

George stepped back from the microphone. The two looked at each other, uncertain about what to do next. Rick stepped up to the microphone in his place.

"Any questions?" he asked.

A man with a shaved head and UFC T-shirt stretching across his gym-swollen body raised a hand.

"You there." Rick pointed at him.

"Have you collected your fifty-dollar bet yet?" the man asked.

Laughter filled the audience.

"You know what, I haven't." He turned to George. "Pay up, bitch."

George reddened as he stepped up to the microphone. "That was a stupid first question."

He took out his wallet and started counting out cash. The crowd chanted every dollar increase. The count stopped at forty-five dollars.

"What the hell? He didn't have all the money

in the first place," Rick said.

The audience burst into laughter.

"Well, you didn't seem to mind when I bought that twelve pack." George looked around wildly, then behind him. His eyes narrowed on Karl. "Double or nothing, Karl over here still has his natural curlies."

Rick sized up Karl whose face had drained to a ghostly white.

"You're on, Cuz."

They pounced on Karl, who was starting to edge away from the group. He shouted a meager "No!" as he was wrestled to the ground. Seconds later, Karl's pants and silk boxers were yanked down around his ankles. The audience of several hundred men leered at the exposed lawyer.

"Son of a bitch," George swore.

On that day, the Pantsin' Party was born. A few years later the party would go on to sweep elections throughout the country. Karl's silk boxers were enshrined at the entrance of the Pantsin' headquarters and considered by many to be a national treasure. Anthropologists would later pinpoint the rally as the point when America's "Great Experiment" had run its course.

The Whitest Boy On The Block

Paul Heatley

RON WAITS FOR THE bus to pick him up.

He feels watched. The prison is behind him, its barred windows like eyes, its double-wide entrance its mouth. It calls him back. He won't listen. He won't turn.

He hears the low rumble of a car's engine idling by the curb down the road. Ron closes his eyes, hoping it doesn't approach.

It does.

He doesn't need to see inside to know who it is.

Scab leans out the passenger window. He wears a vest to show the tattoos that run up his arms, over his shoulders, and around the back of his neck to the top of his head. Norse gods, 18's, Jesus crucified, and, close to his forehead sitting inside a medallion design, a swastika. Scab grins. There are teeth missing.

"How does it feel, Ron?" he asks.

Ron nods. "It feels good."

Scab reaches out, squeezes his arm. "Shit, man, you got *big*."

"So did you."

Scab flexes, then tilts his head toward the backseat. "Get in."

Ron looks past Scab to the driver, Toksvig. Toksvig glances back at him, then turns away. He is a big man, bigger than Ron and Scab put together, so big he barely fits behind the steering wheel. The tattoos on his knuckles alternate between iron crosses and swastikas.

"I was gonna take the bus," Ron says.

"Bowers sent us to get you."

Ron stiffens at the name, hopes it isn't obvious. "I'll catch him tomorrow."

"He'd rather it's today."

Ron looks down the road. The bus isn't coming.

"He's missed you, brother. You and him got a lot to talk about. He wants to see how you liked it. He told you he'd take care of you, right?"

"I'll wait for the bus."

Scab makes a sound like a growl in the back of his throat, and he struggles to keep the smile on his face. He's getting impatient. "No, man, uh-uh, not gonna work. Bowers wants to see you *today*."

"Something planned?"

Scab looks past him, to the prison. "Maybe. For fuck's sake, get in."

Ron draws a deep breath through his nose. He opens the back door, grabs his bag and throws it inside, then climbs in after. Toksvig looks at him in the mirror, grunts, then pulls away.

Scab twists in his seat. He wraps his hand round Ron's jaw and turns his face to the right. On the left side of Ron's neck there's a big swastika. They'd made him prove himself inside, branded him afterward to announce his initiation into the Brotherhood. Scab whistles. "Nice," he says. "How long'd it take?"

"Coupla months. CO's spotted it. They got pissed."

Scab laughs. "What'd they do?"

"Spent a few days in solitary."

"But you persevered, brother. Awesome."

"Yeah." Ron closes his eyes, puts his head back. "Awesome."

***

The inside of Bowers' home hasn't changed much in the intervening years. The living room is kept neat—two sofas, a television in the corner, and there is a bookshelf filled with *Mein Kampf*, *Hunter*, *The Camp of the Saints*, and *The Turner Diaries*. He has multiple copies of each for distribution purposes. The kitchen walls are decorated with defaced posters of Martin Luther

King Jr, Malcolm X, Al Sharpton, and Barack Obama, each with scratched out eyes and swastikas over their faces. A well used dartboard on the back of the door has a picture of Huey P. Newton pinned to it.

Bowers sits at the table, smoking. When he smiles he runs his tongue over his teeth.

"There he is," he says. He slaps the flat of his hand on the table top. "And look how he's grown." Bowers gets to his feet, wraps his arms around Ron and squeezes him. "Whoah, there," he says, pulling back so their noses are inches apart. The cigarette is in the corner of his mouth. The smoke blows into Ron's face. "Can't get my arms all the way round you, hoss!"

Ron feels boxed in by Scab and Toksvig behind him. Bowers holds him for longer than necessary. He has a 1488 tattooed under his right eye, and two black teardrops under his left. He only had one when Ron went inside.

"They take care of you?"

"Yeah."

Bowers lets go now, reaches out and traces the swastika on Ron's neck. "Good. Told you, didn't I?"

"Yeah."

"Looks like they bulked you up, too. Toughened you as well, I bet. Remember when I first laid eyes on you?" He leans past Ron, talks to the others. "Remember what this kid looked like? He was thinner than you, Scab!"

"Looked like a glass of milk with legs," Scab says.

Bowers laughs. "The whitest boy on the block. And so shy. First time your momma dragged you out the bedroom to meet me, you looked like you might burst into tears."

Ron says nothing.

"But look at you now. Shit, we shoulda taken one of them before and after shots." Bowers sits back down. He taps ash from the end of his cigarette. "I sent the boys here to pick you up." He motions for Ron to take the chair opposite. "Didn't want you ridin' on no fuckin bus."

"I was gonna go see my mom."

Bowers sucks his teeth. "Ain't much to see."

"Still want to see it."

"Were you gonna lay flowers?"

"I hadn't decided."

"There's nothin to see there. Don't waste your time. One grave's the same as the next." Bowers stubs out the cigarette. "You couldn't go to the funeral?"

"No."

"You didn't miss much there, either."

"You went?"

"Watched them lower her down, yeah. Her sisters cried, her mother cried, her father looked like he didn't know what the fuck was goin' on." Bowers laughs. Scab joins in. Toksvig goes to the window, looks out, taciturn as ever. "He's dead now too, your grandfather. You hear about that?"

"No."

"Well shit, I figured they woulda told you. Went in his sleep. Just stopped breathin'. He got cremated, though. That's the way to do it."

Ron stares into the ashtray.

Bowers lights another cigarette and smokes in silence for a while, watching Ron. "You understand why she had to die, right?"

Ron nods without looking up. "Yeah."

"If I betray my brother, my life is forfeit."

"She wasn't a brother."

"Still goes."

Bowers gets the attention of Scab and Toksvig, indicates for them to leave. They exit the kitchen, return to the living room. Ron hears them put on the television.

"Ask."

"How'd she go?"

"Quickly."

"You do it?"

He taps the second teardrop. "It brought me no satisfaction. I hope you understand that. I loved your mom, but it had to be done. She betrayed us, she betrayed me—she betrayed *you*, her only son."

Ron knows this isn't true. When she went to the police, she never mentioned his name. She said Bowers' name, and Scab's name, and Toksvig's–but she never said his. "How'd you kill her?"

Bowers stubs out the second cigarette. "You

wanna know?"

"I asked."

"Shot her. Back of the head. Two taps."

"She know you were there?"

"She was sleeping."

Ron nods, but he doesn't believe it.

"So," Bowers says, "tell me."

"Ask me."

"The initiation."

"They left it a few weeks."

"They was getting a feel for you. Checking you out."

"Uh-huh. Sure, they checked me out. First night there, the Brotherhood got me in a cell with one of their biggest guys. Taller than me. That whole first night, he just watched. I didn't sleep."

"Sizin you up, I reckon. You weren't much to look at back then. Nothin on you. Height, sure, but no width. Like a fuckin rake. They needed to know what you were made of."

"Yeah. Well. This guy, he just stared. He didn't sleep either. He wanted me. I could see the hunger in his eyes." Ron remembers those eyes, like a dog that has been told to stay with a full bowl right in front of its nose.

"He fuck you?"

"No."

"You sure?"

"Yes."

"What was his name?"

"It doesn't matter. He didn't fuck me."

"So what happened?"

"For a few weeks all he did was watch. They let me sit with them in the mess hall, and out in the exercise yard, because of you. But they didn't speak to me. Then one day one of them comes over, puts something in my hand, and points at a black guy."

"A shiv."

"Yeah."

"What kind?"

"The shaft of a screwdriver, the handle snapped off. I looked at him and I said 'When?' And he said 'You got a week, then you're on your own.' So there it was. Do or die. It wasn't just the Brotherhood with hungry eyes. Felt like everyone was licking their lips."

"When'd you do it?"

"End of that week. That guy gave me the shiv, he came up, told me 'Tick tock'. I said I was gonna do it. He smiled, went and got a coupla other guys, told me how it was gonna go down. They made a distraction, I went up behind the guy and stuck it in the side of his neck. He dropped. I ran, pushed the screwdriver down into the dirt in the middle of the yard. They didn't find it."

"You were in."

"Yeah."

"When'd they mark you?"

"Started it a couple of weeks later. They didn't wanna do it the same night, it would draw attention."

"After that?"

"After that I counted days."

"You did what they told you?"

"Yeah."

"That's my boy. They bulked you up?"

"Yeah."

The truth was, Ron bulked himself up. The Brotherhood kept him safe, but he didn't trust them, and he didn't want to rely on them.

"Glad you're back, Ron. I missed you. We've all missed you."

Ron nods.

"You're like a son to me, kid. Tore me up when you went away. I been countin' the days, too."

"That means a lot."

"I did what I could for you."

"I know."

"We got somethin goin' down tonight."

"I figured."

"Hell, look at it as a welcoming gift. Your initiation back into *our* fold."

"Sure."

"Tomorrow, we'll get you somewhere of your own. Scab knows a place in town, just down the road from his."

"Great."

Bowers nods, eyes him. "You're outta prison now, but you ain't free. Ain't none of us free, Ron, you know that. You ready to take back up the good fight?"

Ron grits his teeth. "Yeah."

"The war ain't over yet. Nowhere near."

"What's happening tonight?"

"Just a skirmish. Come with me." Bowers gets to his feet and Ron follows. They leave the kitchen, go down the hall to the bedroom. There is a bag on the bed. Bowers opens it, holds it wide for Ron to see inside. It holds two baseball bats and a few handguns. "It's a barn outside of town. There's a punk band playing, some young guys. One of our brothers over the state line got into a fight at one of their shows and they stomped him down. Broke his legs and jaw, cracked his sternum. He's still laid up. Tonight we're gonna meet up with some other brothers and get them at the show." Bowers grins. His teeth are shark-like. "Sound good?"

Ron stares at the bats. He nods.

Bowers grabs his shoulder, squeezes it. "I got somethin else to show you." They leave the bedroom, go to the spare room next door. Bowers pushes the door wide. The thin curtains are drawn, but they let in enough light to see the pale girl with dyed-black hair lying on the bed. She props herself up as they enter, bites her lip ring.

She tilts her chin, speaks to Bowers. "This him?"

"This is him, darlin."

The girl rubs her long legs together. Her feet are bare, painted black toe nails. Her boots are on the floor next to the bed. She pulls down the top of her short dress, exposes her breasts. Her pierced nipples have been tattooed into the shape of swastikas, both of them. She runs her tongue along her bottom lip.

Bowers slaps Ron on the back. "Take your time." He flashes those shark teeth again, then checks his watch. "But not too long. You got until six, then it's my turn. We leave at seven."

"I'm comin' too," the girl says.

Bowers shrugs. "Sure thing, darlin." He looks at Ron, winks, then pushes him into the room.

***

Ron watches the television with Scab and Toksvig. His bag, the one he left prison with, is still in the back of the car. It doesn't have much in it, just some old clothes he doesn't fit into anymore, but there is a picture of his mother holding him as a baby.

Ron was fifteen when she met Bowers. She'd had boyfriends before, but they were few and far between. They had little to do with Ron, and Ron stayed out of their way. Bowers was different. Bowers had more interest in Ron than he had in his mother.

For her part, she knew Bowers was involved in some criminal stuff, she just didn't know the full extent. Small-time, she thought. She didn't know he was a white supremacist yet, he'd only had the one teardrop tattoo. They were together a few years before she found out everything else he was mixed up in. About his crew. The intimidation, the extortion, the violence. The guns he'd taken to hiding in her house.

The guns Ron had been helping him to hide.

By then Ron was in deep. He'd read *Mein Kampf*, and all the other books and pamphlets Bowers passed him on the sly. He knew the story of the teardrop tattoo. He knew how to handle a gun. He knew all about the superiority of the white race.

His mother lost her mind when she realized what Ron had become. She told Bowers she didn't want to see him around again or she'd call the cops.

But Bowers didn't stop seeing Ron. When she found out about that, she went to the cops, like she said she would. It was the worst thing she could have done. Ron took the fall.

He remembers the way she clung to him when the police came to take him away, the way she collapsed in the doorway as the cruiser pulled down the road.

He wasn't shocked when he heard that she'd been murdered. He'd known it was coming. It happened a year into his incarceration. He hadn't cried. You couldn't ever let them see you cry.

"Excited?" Scab says.

Ron blinks. "For what?"

"Tonight."

"Sure."

In the spare room, the headboard knocks

against the wall. The girl cries out. Scab laughs. "She's a loud one, ain't she?"

Ron can still feel her fingernails down his back, on his chest and arms. She'd drawn blood.

Toksvig turns up the volume on the television and switches the channel. A black talk show host appears on screen. Toksvig and Scab flip him the bird, then turn it over.

The headboard bangs like cell doors slamming shut. The girl's moans remind him of the sobs of the raped.

He stands. "I need to piss."

Scab looks at him. "You need someone to hold your hand?"

Toksvig glares at the television. His hands are balled into fists. He looks ready to explode, but he always looks like that. Ron has seen him roar when he fights, like a bear. It is as close as he comes to conversing.

Ron creeps past the spare room in the hallway, but he doesn't go into the bathroom. Instead, he goes into Bowers' bedroom, into the bag on the bed there. He takes out a pistol and checks to be sure it's loaded, then tucks it down his waistband and picks up a bat. He spins it, feels the weight in his hands. He gives it a practice swing.

He keeps the bat low by his side, concealed by his leg. In the spare room they're still fucking. He hopes the headboard and her screams will cover the noise.

"You manage without me?" Scab says, not looking back at him.

"Yeah, I managed," he replies.

Ron steps behind Toksvig first, swings the bat at his head. The impact is so great the bat snaps. Toksvig slumps, then falls out of the chair. Reverberations run up and down Ron's arms, but he keeps a grip on the splintered, jagged handle.

The headboard bangs.

Scab jumps to his feet, eyes wide. He looks from Ron to Toksvig and back again. Blood runs from Toksvig's skull. He's still breathing, but barely.

Scab snaps back into himself. "*Motherfucker!*" he shouts.

He lunges for Ron, arms outstretched. Ron lets him come, watches as he leaps over the sofa and impales himself through the neck on the splintered handle of the bat.

Scab's roar chokes off in his throat. He gurgles, looks shocked. Ron puts a hand on his face and pushes him away, pulling the handle out. Scab falls backward over the sofa and hits the ground next to Toksvig. The blood spraying from his neck covers both downed men. Ron thinks of his initiation in the prison, of the way the blood dripped down the chain-link fence they'd been standing next to. He remembers watching from his cell as the CO's sprayed it off.

The headboard bangs.

Ron drops the handle. Scab gargles. His legs kick, his back arches, but his movements are slowing. Ron grabs a cushion from the sofa. He rolls Toksvig onto his back and holds the cushion over his face. He watches Scab die while he smothers the big man.

When they're both still, he pulls out the gun and heads to the spare room. The headboard still bangs. He opens the door and shoots the girl first, cuts her off mid-scream. He gets her in the shoulder, the bullet skimming Bowers' right arm, making him lose balance and fall from the bed. The girl screams as Ron shoots again. He hits his target this time. The back of her skull paints the headboard.

Bowers sits on the ground now, holding up both hands. "Ron, don't do this," he says, trying to sound calm even though the girl's blood is splattered across his face. "You're making a mistake."

Ron says nothing.

"Ron, you can't kill me. We're brothers. You *know* this, damn it! You kill me, you'll be running the rest of your life!"

"I already killed two brothers. And hell, what's she?" He motions to the body on the bed. "A sister?"

Bowers bites his lip. "I can smooth this over, brother. Trust me. Just put the gun away. Listen to me–put the gun away."

"You killed my mother."

"She sent you to prison!"

"No, she didn't. You did."

"Put the fucking gun down, Ron."

"Was she asleep?"

Bowers frowns. "What?"

"My mother. When you killed her. Was she asleep?"

Bowers bites hard. "No."

Ron raises the gun.

"Don't, Ron. I said you were like a son to me, and I fucking meant that. Don't do *this*."

"I ain't your fuckin son. I ain't your brother, either."

Ron aims for the second tear drop and pulls the trigger. The bullet tears a big enough hole he can't be sure if he was on target.

Bowers hits the ground, bleeding heavily. It spreads around his head the same way Toksvig's did. Ron empties the clip into his body.

He goes through Bowers' wardrobe and finds a jacket he can wear. He puts it on and pulls up the collar. Outside, he gets his bag from the back of the car. He takes out the folded photograph of his mother, puts it in his chest pocket, and walks the two blocks to the bus stop.

Dirty South Of Heaven

Allen Griffin

Tyre and I were about to burst through the front door and get shit going when we heard the crying and pulled up short on the porch.

"Fuck you!" screamed a girl's voice as a door slammed shut. We sweated in the oppressive Saturday afternoon Austin heat. After a moment of quiet, Tyre nodded and we entered the front door as if we'd forgotten to knock.

As we stepped inside, a man in stained boxers walked in from another room and went wide-eyed at the sight of our nickel-plated nines. He held his hands up and began to shake, his belly doing an obscene counter-rhythm where it hung over his underwear's elastic waist band. Tyre nodded toward the hallway to my right. I went into it and began to work my way room to room.

The first door was the shitter. Beyond that were two closed doors across from each other. The room on the left was what passed for a master bedroom, not much more than blackout curtains and a computer with a pornographic screensaver scrolling across the screen. The second room held a girl with her jaw hanging open and one eye that looked like it was starting to swell shut.

I won't lie, the sight of her brought the sounds of explosions to my ears. My Dad had always told me the same thing happened to him the first time he laid eyes on my mother. He'd been a demolition expert in Nam.

His only two loves were Mom and dynamite. But this girl, I'm not sure if she was old enough for me to be hearing anything other than 'run away!'

"Who the fuck are you?" she asked. I shot her a look that usually put people in their place. She just glared back. I tried not to let my composure slip.

"Computer's back here," I yelled back down the hall.

"You guys are Meachy's boys ain't you?" she continued. "Hell, I think I recognize you from working security at a Trill Capone show."

"Why don't I just give you my address and phone number too?" I said.

She returned my sarcasm with a laugh that looked out of place on her face with the shiner.

Tyre pushed the fat dude down the hall with

his nine pressed to the back of his skull. They disappeared into the master bedroom.

"Where do you keep the pictures?" Tyre shouted at him.

I edged into the hallway where I could see the girl and the computer screen. The screensaver disappeared and the fat man opened a folder and typed in a password. Pictures appeared on the screen of various girls in a state of undress. They all looked too young, teenagers at most. I recognized the girl sitting on the bed in some of them.

"Fucking pervert," I yelled into the room.

"No shit," Tyre yelled back. "That's why we're fucking here."

Another picture came up. Brandi, Meachy's niece.

"That's it," Tyre said. A moment later, he cracked the fat dude across the back of the skull. The weight of his body hitting the floor reverberated through the house.

I looked back at the girl. She looked me dead in the eyes but I noticed fear creeping around the edges of her expression.

"How old are you?" I asked.

"Seventeen."

"Who is he to you?" I continued.

"My Dad."

"Jesus fucking Christ."

Tyre shoved a virus-laden thumb drive into one of the computer's ports, something Meachy gave to us that would wipe the hard drive clean. Tyre pressed a couple of buttons and waited for the program to do its thing. When the screen went black, he pulled the tower into the middle of the floor and stomped it to pieces with his big black boots. The fat guy moaned, trying to find his way back to consciousness.

"What's your name?" I asked the girl.

"Angel."

"Do you want to stay here or do you want to go with us?" The wheels started turning in her head doing some kind of math. The fat man sat up, but the look in his eyes said he didn't know shit from Shinola yet.

"Your porn business is done," Tyre said, placing his gun back on the man's skull. The fat man winced as the barrel pressed against the growing welt.

"Stay here," I said to Angel. I pulled a small stick of dynamite out from the waistband beneath my T-shirt. I shoved it into his mouth before he had a chance to react.

"Fuck …" Angel said under her breath.

It really wasn't much more than a glorified firecracker, but it packed a punch psychologically.

I held my flaming Zippo just beneath the wick. The man had terrified eyes as he tried to say something, but it just came out as gibberish. It didn't matter what he had to say anyway.

"If you come near Brandi or Angel or any

other young girl ever again, the next one of these goes in your ass. *Comprende*?" I said.

He nodded his head.

"Let's bounce," Tyre said.

I yanked the stick from his mouth and we headed back down the hall. When we reached the front door, Tyre stopped and gestured at Angel.

"We ain't taking her," he said.

"Yes we are," I said. He knew me well enough to know I meant it. Angel looked back and forth between us. Tyre opened the door and walked out. I nodded to her to follow.

***

Tyre didn't speak on the way to drop us off at my car. He was pissed at me, but he'd get over it. I opened the passenger door for Angel and then got in the other side and drove away to find a hotel room to hole up in. While she got settled in, I went to the liquor store. I kinda figured she'd be gone when I got back, but she was still there.

We stayed up that night and drank and talked. She kissed me but I stopped her there. She would be eighteen soon enough. Even though I worked muscle for Meachy, I still considered myself somewhat of a moral person.

"You really want to wait?" she asked. "You stickin' around that long?"

I was drunk, so I told her about the explosions in my head. She seemed to like it.

I told her about my music and how everyone

called me "Country," even though I played the blues. It all sounded old-timey to her. Said I was the only black guy she knew who was into that shit, wanted to know how I could work security at Trill Capone shows if I didn't like Southern Rap.

"I play music for old souls," I told her. "You know, when like you look back and even the good parts kinda hurt."

"What does Trill play then?"

"Hymns for fucked up youth."

She burst out laughing. "Yeah, shit ... I like that."

She told me her deal too. Parents divorced, Mom ran off with some business guy and lived in Tulsa now. She bounced back and forth for a little while but her Mom lost interest. Pops worked for the Clancy brothers, small time meth dealers running their own little network. Meachy didn't fuck with Meth, but somehow he and the brothers kept stepping on each other's toes. This little side porn business they had, the shit with Meachy's niece, was gonna blow the whole thing wide open.

Angel used to get down with Mark Clancy. When they split, Mark told her Dad to put her in the business, so he did. Some fucked up shit. By the end of that first night, we'd promised to take care of each other. I told her we could set shit straight with the Clancys if she wanted, then move up to Nashville so I could work on my music. She said she was down. Desperate souls always move fast.

***

Meachy called me a couple days later. I knew it was coming, I was just surprised it took so long. I met him at a little dive off South Congress. He sat alone at the table, but I saw a couple of the guys who I worked with at Capone's shows hanging out at the bar top.

As I approached, Meachy stood up and gave me a hearty embrace. He was one of the few men big enough to wrap his arms around me at damn near six foot ten, decked out in a purple silk shirt and puffy tan pants. He looked like he should be in Bell Biv Devoe, not that anyone would tell him that.

"What's good?" I asked as we sat down.

"Look man, Tyre told me about the other day," Meachy replied.

"What can I say?" I shrugged. "The girl's for real. Just how it is, ya know?"

Meachy raised two fingers up in the air and the waitress brought over two tall Shiners and two shots of tequila. We each took a shot and sipped on the beer. He sat silent for a couple of minutes, watching the cars roll by in the blazing sunlight. I don't know if he was thinking about what I said, or if he already knew that I was gonna say it.

"Look, you've always been a good soldier, but

I can't have one of my crew running around with some white girl jailbait. Shit's bad for business."

"I hear you. Hope you understand if I have to go, though."

"I feel you. I always figured one day you'd move on."

"You gonna fuck up the Clancy brothers?"

"I'm working on some shit right now."

"So here's the thing," I started. "I want to help before I go."

Meachy took a long drink from his beer, nodded for me to continue.

"I want to get at Mark, plus I need a little money for the fresh start."

"How much?"

I said a number, a figure I thought was asking too much.

"It's yours, I'll even front it. I trust you."

We shook hands and finished our beers in silence.

***

The next morning we staked out Angel's Dad's place until he left, then broke in to grab some of her stuff. She was scared the cops would be looking out for her as a runaway, but I told her the last thing her old man wanted to do was talk to the cops.

He'd changed the locks but she always kept one of the basement windows unlatched. Angel crawled inside and let me in the back door. I stood watch while she gathered up some things and threw them in an old gym bag.

She held up a driver's license and handed it to me. I could tell it was fake, but it wasn't too bad. I handed it back to her.

"Just in case," she said. Angel could already pass for twenty-one. I didn't know if that made me feel any better, a little less guilty at best. I told myself she was an old soul to ease my discomfort.

A new unopened computer box sat on the floor of her Dad's bedroom. Just for good measure I opened it up and pissed all over the computer tower. Fuck that dude. Angel had asked me not to hurt him, but she laughed whenever she thought about me shoving the dynamite in his mouth, how he'd probably pissed himself.

We loaded up the stuff and headed back to the hotel. I'd already grabbed my stuff from my apartment. We spent the day smoking weed and watching television. She loved to talk shit about the people on those fake court shows. I stayed too stoned too care. Eventually, we fell asleep.

I woke to Angel singing in the shower. It was a Trill Capone tune I knew from working his shows. I liked it better coming from her. The clock on the night stand said it was almost eight.

"What do you think?" she asked when she came out of the bathroom. Armed with access to her wardrobe, she wore a tight black-and-white mini-dress, something Mark Clancy wouldn't be able to resist. In fact, I struggled a bit myself.

"To the nines, girl. He's gonna lose his goddamn mind."

"Still sure you want to wait?" She smiled.

"One more day," I replied, shaking my head.

I didn't know what difference a day or two made in reality. Even her turning eighteen wouldn't close the fifteen-year-plus gap between us, but it was legal, at least.

She didn't wait for me to answer, just went back in the bathroom and finished putting on her makeup. If she was nervous, it didn't show. I loaded our stuff into the car. No good reason to stick around after tonight.

We took the toll road up to Round Rock and hunted down some sports bar Angel said Mark Clancy liked to hang out, a place which sat nestled in a strip mall that used car salesmen liked to go after the dealership closed.

Angel kissed me hard, then strode across the parking lot like she owned the world. There were explosions in my head again. Bile rose in my stomach at the prospect of sitting in the car and waiting for her to seduce her ex. I watched as the bouncer stopped her and she produced her fake ID. Apparently, she needed it after all.

Damned if it didn't seem to take forever. I sat outside smoking Swishers and listening to Lonnie Johnson, so good it hurt. He sang and played guitar and you could hear his kids playing around in the background and I thought about how far away I was from that. I lived south of heaven and I could see no light that wasn't neon. I'd take my pain out on Mark Clancy before the sun rose tomorrow. Maybe I'd see a new light for the first time then.

Angel and Mark emerged from the bar after a couple of hours. Mark stumbled toward his Mustang with her leading him by the hand as he searched his pocket for his keys with the other. He found and then dropped them. She picked them up but didn't give them back. Instead, she pinned him against the door and started making out with him.

I pulled my nine out and felt its weight in my hand. I wanted to say screw the plan and ice him right there. I tried to justify the urge, thinking he was too drunk to drive back to his house, would probably get Angel killed somewhere along the way. Before I lost my nerve, she pushed him in behind the wheel and then snaked around and got in the passenger side.

I started the car. He pulled out and took off too fast down the street, only remembering to turn the lights on after a couple of blocks. I trailed at a safe distance just in case.

They made it to Mark's place and I pulled over down the street to wait for her to unlock the back door so I could rob him. Hopefully that would get us enough cash to start a new life with. She didn't know that Meachy had paid me. I figured she would get over that, especially after what Mark and her Pops had done to her.

I waited fifteen minutes, then grabbed my gun and made my way over to the house. I hopped the chain link and snuck around the back. I peeked in through the kitchen window and didn't see them. I checked the knob to the backdoor, but it was still locked.

"Shit," I muttered to myself. I thought about breaking in, but it was probably too soon. I looked around the back porch for a place to hide. That's when I heard the gunshots.

"Fuck it."

The door gave after two massive kicks and I dashed in, gun drawn. I went room to room, until I found Mark Clancy's corpse lying in his bed, stripped down to his boxers. Two to the head, Angel above him in her underwear, a revolver still smoking in her hand.

I've seen first-time killers before. They usual look shell-shocked, like they're trying to comprehend the finality of what they've just done. Angel had no such look. She looked … satisfied. I ran to her out of instinct. She swung the gun around to me and pulled the trigger again. The bullet grazed my leg and I let out an animal growl.

"What the fuck?" I yelled at her.

"Who do you think you are?" she screamed at me. "You're just like the rest of them, no better."

"Baby, no …" I started to say, but she cut me

off.

"You think a few days makes a big difference, somehow you're in the clear because I'll be eighteen?" She waved the gun around wildly. I thought about taking the gun away from her before she shot me, but it would mean nothing if she still wanted to. Instead,

I held my hands up in submission, hoping this moment would pass, that anger was clouding her mind. But as I approached she pointed the gun at me again and I backed down.

"Mark's dead. Maybe you should be next. I bet I could take Dad out too before the cops found me."

"Angel, just calm down and let me help you. You don't want to mess up and go to jail for murder."

"Who's gonna lock me up after what I've been through?" she snarled.

I didn't have an answer to that. The weight of the situation hit me full force then, and for a moment I thought maybe she should pull the trigger, like maybe I wanted her to. I still had my gun but I felt no desire to defend myself.

"Get up," she hissed. I stood, my leg burning but still able to support my weight. She pointed toward the door with the gun. I hobbled out with her following. We went to my car. I looked around but didn't see any neighbors watching. There were sirens in the distance but it was hard to tell if they were for us. We didn't stick around to find out.

I wondered how much of this Angel had planned. Could her errant shot have been meant to graze my left leg so I could still drive? Of course not. No one was that good. Maybe it was luck, or destiny, which seemed even more absurd, but no more absurd than hearing explosions in your head when you meet your underage soulmate.

"Where are we going?" I asked.

"Go to Dad's."

I knew she was going to say that.

"Look, I'm sorry for everything," I said. "I … I thought you felt about me the way I do about you."

"I don't know," she said. "Maybe I do."

My heart skipped a beat, but I pushed the feeling out. I needed to focus on the issue at hand, which was our need to get out of town.

"If you take me to my Dad's, we'll leave town right after, I promise," she finally said. "I'm sorry … I don't trust anyone, not even you, but I'm trying."

"Maybe we should let things die down for a while and then come back for him," I said. Honestly, I figured if I could get her to leave now she'd never come back. The night was running with its own momentum, a lit fuse on a stick of dynamite. It was now or never if we were going to go together.

"No," she said. "Let's go to Dad's."

The dilemma must've been obvious in my expression.

"He's got money, enough money you could record your first album on your own," she said.

"Then why didn't you just take it when we went to get your stuff?" I replied.

"Because it's in a safe. But don't worry, I've got a plan."

The best laid plans … I knew a shit storm when I saw one, but there was no turning back at this point, at least if I wanted to have any chance with Angel.

***

We pulled up near her father's and left the motor running. I took my pistol out from its holster, showing her it wasn't meant for her. She motioned for me to put it away. I wanted to tell her she didn't have to do this, but maybe she did need to do it. Maybe gunning down her own father was the only way to get out from beneath the shit storm she'd been born into. I watched her run up to the house and knock on the door. I saw the shaft of interior light slowly light her up when the door opened. Then she raised her hands out in front of her and screamed "No!"

The shotgun's blast left little doubt of the cause. I cried out. The explosions in my head were real this time, no doubt.

I leapt from the car and ran toward her. Her father stepped onto the porch and stood over her body. He didn't seem to notice me as he aimed the second barrel down at her. He might have been crying, but I didn't take the time to find out. I emptied my clip in his direction. I'm not sure how many times I hit him, but it was enough.

When I reached the porch there wasn't enough left of her face to recognize the girl I'd known three minutes before. I pulled the shotgun away from her father's twitching hands and put the second barrel to his head. When I pulled the trigger there was even less of him left. I don't remember leaving, but somehow I knew I'd never forget. Sometimes a night, or even just a moment can be frozen in time, like a classic blues song, echoing out of the past.

I never knew why her Dad was waiting, why he did what he did. Had he somehow got tipped off about Mark Clancy, or maybe he was just sick, heart broken by his daughter running away.

Sometimes, the ones that love you the most are the ones who do the most damage.

The Contractors

David A. Anthony

A COOL AFTERNOON RAIN pattered against the windows as Rico Garcia glanced about the old man's living room, making mental note of everything that was here. He had a decent TV — a 40-incher, Sony — and a Blu-ray player, but nothing more extravagant. The old man seemed to live a frugal lifestyle. But he'd once been an attorney and attorneys had money, regardless of what was evident here. Maybe most of it was in the bank or in various investments, but an old guy like this might have some of it stashed under his mattress or in a safe in the closet, too. He'd need to search the place to be sure.

"Does it look okay?" the old guy asked. "I only use real wood. None of that synthetic crap. What do you think?"

Rico blinked at the old man, momentarily

confused by his question. Then he remembered he was posing as a fireplace inspector for the condominium complex. Today was the day that residents were required to open their doors for the homeowners association's mandatory yearly inspection. Signs had been posted all over the grounds for the last two weeks. The real inspector was tied up inside one of the other apartments.

"Yeah," Rico said. "Looks good. You take real nice care of it." He looked again at the fireplace, feigning interest. "Say it's just you here, right?"

"Yes. My wife passed away three years ago. Lung cancer."

Rico shook his head. "Sorry to hear that, amigo. That cancer's a real bitch. Don't discriminate, ya know? The good news is, you'll be seeing her again real soon."

For a moment, the old man just stood there, silent, the only sound the afternoon rain knocking on the windows like a stranger trying to get in. Then a look of horrific realization spread across his face. Before he could utter a word Rico had the gun out and pointed at his head.

"Not a word," Rico said. "Unless you wanna go see her right now."

The old man kept his mouth shut as Rico ushered him into the kitchen, tied and gagged him and obtained his keys. He'd lock the place up and they'd come back after dark with the van, load up the stuff and try to figure out where the old guy kept his cash. It was a good system.

They'd spend weeks searching apartments, condos, and neighborhoods until they found just the right place, at just the right time—an event: a fireplace inspection, alarm upgrade, a mass insect extermination, anything that would force unsuspecting people to allow complete strangers inside their homes without question. They could case a dozen homes in a short time, get the keys, and make sure nobody would be home when they returned to collect their spoils. It was almost too easy.

Rico's phone rang. It was Carlos. "What you got, homie?"

"Nada. Bald dyke ain't got shit. Old ass TV and some ugly men's clothes. You?"

"Not much. Okay TV, maybe some cash. I put him down so we can check it out later."

Carlos huffed out a sigh. "Shit, man. The fuck's up with these people? Ain't nobody here got nothing. We better find some cash or jewels or something or we just wasting our time."

"Be cool, man. There'll be something good. You'll see."

"There better be. I ain't risking going back inside for—hold up! You see this van?"

Damn it, Rico thought. *Not again*. "What are you talking about? What van?"

"The grey one with the tinted windows. Looks like the kind we use. Maybe someone else had the same idea."

"Come on, Carlos. Don't go getting crazy

again. Ain't nothing for us in that van. That's the kinda shit that'll get us locked up."

"I'm just gonna take a quick look. I'll call you back."

The line went dead.

"Fuck," Rico muttered as he put his phone away. He wondered again why he'd brought Carlos in on this. He might be Rico's cousin, but Carlos was unpredictable and dangerous. There was no reason to start breaking into cars. He was bound to get them caught if he kept this up.

Rico got up and exited the apartment, locking the door behind him. He hurried down the stairs and around the corner to the next apartment. Carlos was right about one thing: they needed to hit pay dirt soon. They'd been inside several of the units already and found nothing especially valuable. That wasn't good. They were taking a big risk doing this in broad daylight.

There had better be something here worth putting their hands on.

**

Sonya Jasper walked nervously from room to room in the small condo, listening to the rain coming down outside. It was a gloomy afternoon, as was the case most of the winter here in Seattle, where the sun was held constant prisoner to an endless expanse of gunmetal-grey clouds. It was nothing like San Diego. Not at all like the blistering hot afternoons of her childhood, the bright sunshine and tall palm trees. But today she felt an eerie similarity in the air, that same expectant stillness, the tension wrapping itself around her throat like a cold, clammy hand.

It felt just like the day her mother was killed.

It will be okay, she kept telling herself. They were out there right now, probably already on their way to her doorstep. But it was all set up properly. Help was right outside in the parking lot, waiting for her signal. Still, she felt cold and exposed, wearing only the thin, nearly-transparent slip and a pair of thong panties. She may as well be naked. But that was, of course, the intention. To get them to attack her, and then the cavalry would arrive and save the day.

But this was how her mother had died, back in California, when Sonya was only eight years old. A couple of gangbangers kicked their door down in the middle of the afternoon, coming for cash and electronics but finding only a pretty blonde in her late-twenties, her husband away at work. Taking what they wanted from her instead. Sonya had stayed quiet inside the coat closet until it was over. Which meant she had survived, at least.

But that afternoon had changed her. It made her a harder, colder person. As she grew older it affected her relationships with men, destroyed her ability to trust. She'd even turned to women for a while, but eventually decided she didn't enjoy the taste of pussy. Instead she turned to celibacy — or, more frequently, her vibrator — and concentrated on her need to track down and punish men like those who murdered her mother. She got a degree in criminal justice, joined the Seattle Police Department, and quickly worked her way up to detective.

But something was off this afternoon. Her detective's intuition was setting off alarm bells inside her head, making her pace the rooms, telling her to call it off while she still could.

Stop it, she told herself. It was all going to work out just fine. She'd been trained for this sort of thing; her partner and the others were just outside. Besides, she needed to do this, not just for the people these men were victimizing, but *for herself*. She'd been through plenty of dangerous situations as a beat cop, even more as a detective.

But this one was different, personal. A nightmare from the past that lingered with her, haunted her dreams. She needed to lay it to rest if she ever wanted to move on with her life.

A knock sounded on the front door.

Shit.

Sonya took a deep breath and went to the door, hesitated behind it. "Who is it?" she called through the wood.

"Fireplace inspectors, ma'am."

The voice had a Hispanic accent. Sonya unlocked the door and cracked it open. A man's face stared back at her. He had a dark brown complexion, thin black goatee, and there was something cruel in the wicked curve of his lips.

"You must have the wrong apartment," she said. "I didn't call for any fireplace inspectors."

"Your homeowners association set it up. They should have notified you we were coming today. There's fliers all over the complex. We have to do your yearly inspection. It should only take a minute, but it's mandatory."

Mandatory? They were really pushing their authority here, forcing their way in. Her backup sure as hell better be ready for her signal.

Sonya pulled the door the rest of the way open and stepped back to let him inside. A cold breeze preceded him in and Sonya had an impulse to pull her robe tighter around her, realized she wasn't wearing one, and felt a sudden spike of icy panic race through her veins. She could feel her erect nipples sticking out through the thin fabric of the slip, knew that he could see them too. His shoulder brushed against them as he pushed his way inside. The door clicking shut behind him sounded like a pistol's hammer snapping back.

"It's right over there," Sonya said, gesturing toward the old brick fireplace.

The man showed no interest in the fireplace. He just stood in the foyer, staring at her, a sick smile on his face. "You look like I caught you just getting out of bed. Some lucky guy in there keep you up all night?"

"I was working late," she lied. "There's no

one here but me."

His grin widened. He glanced around the room, probably noticing the expensive TV, the iPad, the big, fake rock on her left hand—all of it put there to draw his attention.

And it was working.

The man reached behind his back and produced a silencer-equipped pistol, pointing it at her. "That's good. Because you and I are gonna have ourselves a real good time this afternoon. And we wouldn't want anyone interrupting us, now would we?"

*****

"And then she says, 'Do I look like that kind of a girl?' all offended-like. And I say, 'Uh, yeah, in that dress you do. She looks down at the dress, which barely covers her ass, and she says, 'Yeah, I guess you're right,' and then she sucks my dick anyway!"

Omar started laughing almost before the words finished coming out of his mouth. The vibrations made the entire van rock. Quinton cracked a smile and chuckled, but Andy just shook his head, surprised the bald little shit could get a woman to go out with him at all, let alone suck his dick. Andy suspected they were hookers, but Omar would never admit that to a couple of police detectives.

The van was somewhat outdated, but the best they could get on their limited budget, and the so-called 'surveillance expert' that came with it, Omar, even less impressive, in Andy's opinion. They'd been planning this operation for weeks, ever since they got on the trail of the brazen daylight robbery suspects they'd named *The Contractors*, because they always posed as some form of workmen.

Unit F305 belonged to Sally Harwood, an elementary school teacher and mother of two, currently going through a divorce. She'd put the condo on the market and moved back to Idaho two months ago, leaving the place vacant. When the complex came on their radar as a potential target for The Contractors, they'd reached out to Harwood and gotten her permission to use it, then stocked it full of electronics, jewelry, and fine china in an effort to entice the suspects. They'd left credit cards and cash laying out, fake tax documents, and then there was the big temptation, the one Sonya had insisted on, the thing that would get these men's attention even if all the other treasure had not:

Her.

Detective Sonya Jasper was a beautiful woman. Long brown hair, dark grey eyes, and a body most women would kill for. She was also the youngest detective on the force. But it was her determination Andy admired most about her, her dedication to the job, her sense of self-sacrifice. It was incredibly dangerous for Sonya to be going inside by herself. He hated her doing it, but for reasons he couldn't quite understand this operation was intensely personal to her. She was determined to be the one going in. That's why they were out here in the van, using the monitors and listening equipment to watch the hidden cameras they'd set up inside, ready to burst through the door the second she said the code phrase.

"Sounds like you had yourself one hell of a weekend, Omar," Quinton said. "If it's all true, which I seriously doubt."

"Don't be a hater," Omar replied. "You just wish you could get all the little hotties at the club."

"You keep telling yourself that." Quinton turned to Andy. "How about you, Detective Dalton? Any lovely ladies keeping your bed warm these rainy winter nights?"

Andy shrugged. "Not since Amy left."

The young, black detective looked at Omar and they both grinned. "That's not what we hear. Word around the department is you and your partner been getting a little closer than partners are supposed to get."

Andy's face started to redden. "No idea what you're talking about."

"Aww, don't be like that, Dalton," Omar said. "We're all friends here, right? What's discussed in the van, stays in the van. So tell us, what's Detective Jasper like in bed?"

Andy just rolled his eyes. "I wouldn't know."

"Yeah, you do," Quinton said. "I'm a detective, remember? I detect shit … especially *bullshit*. I see the way you look at her. That's more than partners being partners."

Andy opened his mouth to produce another lie, realized it was pointless, and then sighed. "Fine. But this stays in the van. Got it?"

Quinton gave the Boy Scout's salute. "Scout's honor."

"Hell yeah," Omar agreed. "My van's a sacred place. Shit, I wouldn't want you guys telling anyone about my seventeen—err…eighteen-year-old at the club last weekend."

They both glared at him.

"All right," Andy said, sighing again. "Yes, there is something between Sonya and me, but I don't know how serious it is. I wouldn't mind it *getting* serious but I don't think she wants that. She's really hard to read. She doesn't like to let people in."

"Yeah, she can be a real ice queen," Omar replied.

Quinton snorted. "Just because she's shunned *your* advances don't make her an ice queen. Hell, most women do that. Except for teeny-boppers and girls you pay for."

"Damn, Quinton. You cut me deep." Omar pantomimed a stabbing motion toward his chest and pretended to be dead.

"She's not an ice queen," Andy said. "She's just … cautious. Being a female detective is hard."

"Speaking of hard …" Omar glanced at the monitors. Sonya was walking through the house toward the living room, her purple thong showing clearly through the diaphanous material of the slip. "You have no idea what that outfit she's wearing is doing to me right now."

"Fuck you, Omar," Andy said. "That's my partner."

Omar grinned. "Chill out, dude. I'm just fucking with you."

"Anyway," Andy continued, turning back to Quinton. "I think it has to do with her past. Her dad was a detective and a single father, so she was mostly raised by her aunt. I still don't know what happened to her mother. Every time I bring up the subject she shuts down."

"I'm sure she'll tell you when she's ready. Just give her time." Quinton smiled. "I'm happy for you guys. Really. Hope it all works out. She's a great girl and one hell of a detective. Just don't let the chief find out, or you guys won't be partners much longer."

"No kidding," Omar said. "That man's got a stick shoved so far up his—*oh fuck!*"

They all turned back to the monitors to see a young Hispanic man standing in the living room with Sonya, pointing a gun at her. She was saying the phrase meant to trigger their intervention, but none of them had heard her until now. She looked terrified as the man forced her back inside the apartment, shoved her to the ground, and told her to take off her slip.

Panic burned through Andy's veins as he stared at the monitors, witnessing what could be the last few moments of his partner's life. He needed to get in there *right now*. He turned to the back door of the van and reached for the handle …

But the door flew open before he could touch it.

The man standing on the other side looked just as shocked to see them as Andy was to see him. It was Carlos Alvarez, one of the men they were hunting, one of the killers.

Andy reached for his pistol, but Alvarez already had his revolver out and pointed at him. A bolt of pain exploded up Andy's shoulder as the gun went off. He dropped to the van floor in agony. His ears rang. The world sounded muffled and far away, but through the pain and the chaos he heard several more shots. He looked up in time to see a bullet tear through Omar's jaw, shattering it and sending teeth raining down onto the floor of the van. Another burst through his left eye, blowing it to pieces and splattering the monitors and consoles with blood and chunks of brain. Andy heard Quinton fire off several quick shots behind him. The shots went wide and Alvarez returned fire. Quinton screamed and dropped to the ground as the bullets struck him. Warm blood splashed onto Andy's back and neck.

Carlos Alvarez climbed inside the van. The

sun cast him in silhouette. Andy had the sensation of the Grim Reaper himself looming over him. Alvarez looked down and saw Andy was still alive, then grinned manically as he pointed his revolver at Andy for the killing shot. The gun clicked when he squeezed the trigger.

Andy raised his Glock and pointed it at Alvarez, whose face looked shocked.

He squeezed the trigger.

***

"I'm not gonna tell you again, bitch. Take it off."

Sonya had retreated into the living room as far as she could, on her knees in front of the couch. She'd already said the code phrase several times, but to no effect. Where the hell was her backup? Where was Andy? He had to be seeing this. *What were they doing out there?*

She had a 9mm pistol, fully loaded with the safety off, under the cushions at the far end of the couch. She needed to get to it. But Rico Garcia wasn't stupid. He'd see her going for it and kill her. She needed a distraction.

"Okay," she said as calmly and cautiously as she could. "Just don't shoot me." She lifted the slip up over her head and threw it down onto the floor, exposing her bare breasts. Garcia grinned as she did it, and she could see the bulge forming in his pants. She used the movement to slide several more inches to her left toward the weapon.

"Yeah, baby," Garcia said. "That's what daddy likes to see. You got nice titties."

"Thanks," she said, disgusted, but she slid another couple inches to the left.

"Stop moving," he commanded. He glanced down at the other end of the couch. "What you doing? What's down there you trying to get?"

"Nothing. I'm just … terrified. Please don't hurt me." She tried to put on the scared maiden act. Her heart was racing, but it was anger more than fear that dominated her thoughts. In her mind this was one of the men who'd killed her mother. She'd make him pay for it.

"No? How about we take a look, then?" Garcia moved toward the end of the couch, reaching for the cushions. Sonya thought for sure that this was her last chance. She needed to make her move.

The sound of gunshots exploded through the air. Garcia turned toward windows. Sonya saw her chance. She dove to the end of the couch, reached beneath the cushion, and retrieved her pistol.

"Seattle PD," she said, standing and pointing the gun at him. "Drop the weapon, asshole. You're under arrest."

Garcia spun, pointing his own pistol at her. At first he looked shocked, then his eyes landed on her bare breasts and he grinned. "You'd sound a lot tougher if your titties weren't hanging out, bitch. I ain't dropping shit. You drop your gun."

"I don't think so."

They stood there, silent, pointing guns at each other, for what felt like hours. The shooting outside had stopped. The only sounds now were a faint ticking coming from a clock somewhere inside the apartment, and the quiet animal-like hum of the refrigerator. Sonya's hands were starting to sweat on the grip of the pistol. It occurred to her how absurd she must look, a half-naked woman pointing a loaded pistol at him. But she didn't care. She only cared about taking him in or killing him, whichever it came down to.

Another shot rang out in the parking lot. Garcia's head automatically swung toward the sound. His gun hand moved with his body and Sonya took the opportunity to put a bullet in his chest. Garcia winced and dropped to his knees, pulling the trigger of his own gun as he fell. His bullet tore through her right thigh. She hit the floor, screaming, blood starting to gush from the wound now. She'd lost her grip on her pistol, sending it sliding across the floor and under the loveseat.

"You bitch!" Garcia screamed, holding a hand to his bleeding wound. "You fucking bitch!" He tried to raise his gun again but was unable at first. Sonya tried to stand, but pain seared up her leg and she fell back down. She tried again, but by then Garcia was already recovering. He looked up at her with fury in his eyes and his gun in his hand, and she immediately turned and hobbled off toward the kitchen.

Several shots followed her in, and Sonya screamed and dove behind the center island for cover. Pain radiated up her leg and blood smeared across the tile as bullets ricocheted off hanging pots and cabinets. One hit the microwave and it hissed like an angry snake. Sonya frantically opened cabinets and drawers, looking for anything she could use as a weapon. She found a heavy cast-iron frying pan and held it behind her right ear like a baseball player up to bat, then bit her lip and tried to ignore the pain as she waited for Garcia to round the corner.

But Garcia didn't move. He just stood there in the kitchen doorway. "You one crazy-ass cop, you know that? Waiting in here all naked and shit. But that shit didn't work, and now Carlos killed your backup. That's what all that shooting was out there. So you may as well just give up, make this easy on yourself. I promise I won't kill you if you do."

Sonya said nothing. She wasn't stupid enough to give away her position by speaking. Instead she waited, hoping he'd come through the door.

Garcia finally took a step inside the room, his pistol out in front of him. Sonya smashed the frying pan into his face.

Garcia screamed as bone and cartilage shattered and his nose disappeared into his face. He fired his pistol, not aiming, sending chunks of wood exploding from the cabinets. Sonya raised the frying pan over her head and brought it down with a sickening crack.

Garcia stumbled back a few feet, dazed, his eyes wide with shock. Blood flowing from the fresh wound coalesced with the river already flowing from his nose, turning his face into a grotesque red mask. But he stayed on his feet. His gun fell from his hand and his body dropped to the ground.

"Sonya!" Andy stood in the kitchen doorway, his pistol still pointed at the spot where Garcia had been just a moment ago. His shoulder was bleeding.

Sonya tried to go to him but her injured leg went numb and she started to fall. Andy ran to her, catching her before she could hit the ground. He scooped her up and carried her out of the apartment.

To her left Sonya saw the body of the other Contractor, Carlos Alvarez, lying behind the surveillance van in a pool of congealed blood. Andy set her down on the sidewalk and wrapped his coat around her, covering her nakedness. In the distance, sirens screamed like banshees. Residents were starting to emerge from their apartments to see what all the commotion was about. Andy was saying something to her, but she wasn't listening. In her mind, she was already thinking about how it would be different next time. Next time she'd kill them all herself. The men who'd killed her mother were still out there. Maybe she'd eventually find them.

Until then, there were plenty of others who could take their place.